UNDER SIEGE

For Mom and Dad

SHARK WARS

EJ ALTBACKER

THE
Last
Emprex

razOr
bill

An Imprint of Penguin Group (USA) Inc.

razOr
bill

A division of Penguin Young Readers Group
Published by the Penguin Group
Penguin Group (USA) Inc., 345 Hudson Street
New York, New York 10014, U.S.A.

USA / Canada / UK / Ireland / Australia / New Zealand / India / South Africa / China
Penguin Books Ltd, Registered Offices: 80 Strand, London WC2R 0RL, England
For more information about the Penguin Group visit penguin.com

Published simultaneously in Canada

Library of Congress Cataloging-in-Publication Data is available

ISBN: 978-1-59514-544-4

Printed in the United States of America

1 3 5 7 9 10 8 6 4 2

THE Last Emprex

PROLOGUE

GRAY REACHED OUT WITH HIS SENSES AND zipped forward in the cold water to the massive forest of staghorn coral. It was immense, its branches reaching toward the chop-chop. He turned and in a blink was at the other side of the formation. Using shar-kata, Gray could travel the hundred yards between the two ends in a fraction of a tail stroke. Shar-kata was a sharkkind martial art known and mastered by only a very few.

Unfortunately Gray wasn't one of those few.

Most of the time he could travel well and create shields, but that was about it. He couldn't consistently use the power of the waters and bend it to his will or turn it into a destructive force like a true master. Instead, Gray relied on his own natural speed and strength as a megalodon. His species had gone extinct from the oceans millions of years ago. But underneath the Big Blue, below even the deepest part of the Dark Blue, were the Underwaters. This was a pocket of ocean unchanged since the time of Tyro, where jurassic sharkkind and dwellers still lived. Gray had come into the Big Blue from the Underwaters when he was just a pup.

Now, many years later, the jurassics that lived there were threatening the Big Blue.

Gray tried to make light of his shar-kata shortcomings as Takiza shook his head. "I *have* been practicing, I promise. But apparently practice doesn't always make perfect."

Takiza Jaelynn Betta vam Delacrest Waveland ka Boom Boom was his full name and he was a tiny betta, or Siamese fighting fish. Takiza, though a small fish, *was* a shar-kata master. He flicked his billowing, rainbow colored fins, annoyed. "And apparently, sometimes practice doesn't even make barely sufficient. Yes, I can see that while I was away you continued re-learning to swim quickly in a straight line. That will be ever so helpful if Hokuu and Grimkahn decide to hover directly in front of you."

Grimkahn was the mosasaur king, a seventy foot ocean crocodile, who wanted to conquer the Big Blue. And Hokuu had been Takiza's own master. He was an evil frilled shark, thirty feet long with a dangerously spiked tail that could split even the thickest skull. It was Hokuu who had freed Grimkahn and his forces to

2

menace the Big Blue. Just as Gray was Takiza's apprentice, Takiza had been Hokuu's. But that was before the frilled shark had turned evil.

While his master wasn't impressed, Leilani was astonished. The AuzyAuzy spinner shark had never seen Gray use his shar-kata powers. "That's incredible! I mean, I've heard of shar-kata, the legends, how could you not—but to actually watch it in action, wow!"

Gray smiled at Takiza. "See? I got a wow from her."

"Is that why you chose to bring Leilani to the training area?" Takiza asked. "To impress her? How nice."

It seemed to be sheer coincidence that Takiza had passed by this side of Fathomir, but Gray knew the betta far too well to believe that. And he kind of *was* trying to impress Leilani, but of course he would never admit to it. Takiza had returned from searching much of the ocean for Grimkahn and his jurassic horde and found nothing, which was troubling. The mosasaur king wanted more than anything to rule the ocean and send Gray to the Sparkle Blue. But after Gray had miraculously defeated Grimkahn and the jurassics at the Battle of the Spine, they had disappeared into the depths of the vast ocean.

Leilani swished her tail. "With respect, Takiza, that's not fair. I know he's been practicing a lot and this is the first time he asked me along."

"It gets boring by myself," Gray said.

3

"This is serious," Takiza said. "You must progress or you will never defeat Grimkahn and Hokuu."

Leilani added, "The Eyes and Ears have nothing new to report either. And BenzoBenzo has been listening carefully to everything." BenzoBenzo was a giant deep sea blowfish and the head of AuzyAuzy's spyfish unit, the Eyes and Ears. "We do know that Grimkahn *did* return to the Underwaters, though."

Takiza stared thoughtfully at them both. "Yes, but we don't know if they've come back."

"We would know if they were in the Big Blue," Gray said, trying to stay positive. "You would have found some sign. Hopefully they'll think better of trying anything after the whipping we gave them last time around," he added, emphasizing his words with a fin slash.

"I hope you are right," the betta told them. "I really do. But you should not trust the safety of the entire Big Blue to *hoping* things shall work out. You must prepare. Now, use your shar-kata speed and swim through this field of staghorn without breaking any of the branches. . . ."

Takiza waited.

Gray nodded, gritting his teeth. He called for the power of the tides and it came to him, filling his body with energy in the form of pure white sparkles. He could do this. The field was thick but all he had to do was make a few turns and he'd easily pass through.

Gray launched himself forward and ... plowed straight into the staghorn, taking out a swath thirty feet wide. He was a megalodon, after all, so training mistakes tended to cause damage.

After a moment, he swam out, embarrassed. "Oops."

"Well, there goes two hundred years of coral. Since we are hoping, I *hope* you can do better, and soon," Takiza said. "I fear that the situation in the Big Blue may turn for the worse."

Gray was scratched and bruised but he was determined not to let Takiza ruin his optimism. Deep down he *was* worried. But a leader couldn't be frightened of shadows. That made everyone nervous. The seven seas were quiet and he would remain positive. Perhaps Grimkahn had ordered his mariners to stay in the Underwaters.

What was the mosasaur king going to do? Fight the entire Big Blue?

Gray did not know this at the time, but he would bitterly regret not having made more progress in his shar-kata studies during this peaceful time. In fact, the future of the Big Blue would ride on an urchin spine because of it.

THREE MONTHS LATER

CHAPTER 1

"WE ARE CUT OFF, MY FRIENDS," SAID Silversun, the leader of Vortex Shiver. He was a port jackson shark with a blocky head and a mottled, dark brown hide. He was also the smartest sharkkind that Grinder knew. With them was Kendra, the leader of AuzyAuzy Shiver, who had come to their aid earlier with a force of five hundred sharkkind. Their numbers had dwindled rapidly in the fighting. Kendra herself was badly wounded with a deep frilled shark bite below her right fin.

It didn't look like she would survive the battle.

It seemed none of them would.

Grinder gnashed his teeth in frustration. Silversun was totally right. There was no escape. Years ago he would have never asked a port jackson for advice, or any other shark for that matter. Grinder was the leader of Hammer Shiver, the largest force of hammerheads in the Sific Ocean, maybe in the entire wet world. Asking advice was for weaklings. Or so he used to think.

Was I stupid, Grinder thought.

"Nevertheless, we have to face the facts," said Kendra. "This will not go our way." She swirled her long tail with its characteristic white tip. Kendra, Grinder, and Silversun were leaders of the most powerful shivers in the Sific Ocean. A few years ago, if any of their forces had met, there would have been blood. Now, because of the prehistore threat from the Underwaters, they were close allies.

No, it was more than that.

They were friends.

Not that their friendship was making much of a difference at this moment. They were losing badly.

Grinder yelled at one of his subcommanders. "Fix our midsection, Slasher! We're Hammer Shiver, and we're not going down without a fight!"

"Yes, sir!" the shark told him. Slasher began barking orders, shoring up the center of their diamond formation. They had used a pyramid before and were blasted for that effort. Would this formation work better against Grimkahn and his horde of giant mosasaurs and evil-quick frilled sharks?

Grinder's heart sank because he knew the answer.

No. It would not.

"I wish Jaunt was here with the rest of our mariners,"

Kendra said. Jaunt was Kendra's second-in-command, but she was off on the other side of AuzyAuzy territory battling a splinter force of Grimkahn's horde.

"It wouldn't make a difference," Silversun said in a low voice.

"Why haven't they finished us off already?" Grinder asked. "They broke away from their last attack after smashing our formation to pieces."

Silversun flicked his paddle tail back and forth before he answered. "They're taking our measure, I think."

It made sense. The jurassic dwellers from the Underwaters were powerful to begin with, but now they had learned to swim in formation. They had probably been practicing during their absence. The huge mosasaurs, most fifty and sixty feet long with large crocodile mouths, could destroy a battle fin of a hundred sharks by themselves. There were also frilled sharks, or frills, which were twenty and thirty feet long. These eel-like frills were wickedly agile and plugged the holes between the mosasaurs to protect them—all this while launching deadly attacks with their own spiked tails.

Over the last three months this horde had gone on a rampage through the Sific. Grinder, Kendra, and Silversun weren't going to hover idly by and do nothing, and negotiations were pointless. Grimkahn wanted to rule the ocean and would destroy anything in his path. After the jurassic horde tore through AuzyAuzy Shiver's territory, they had come to Hammer and Vortex Shiver waters.

There was nothing to do but fight.

If only Gray and the others at Fathomir were here, then perhaps they might have a chance. Gray was the Seazarein Emprex of the seven seas. He alone could bring together all the shivers and then maybe, just maybe, they would have a chance. But there was no way to get word to Gray in time. Grimkahn's horde had appeared out of nowhere.

"They're playing with us," Grinder spat.

"Yes," Kendra said. "And they're gaining valuable information about what to expect when they attack Gray and his forces." She winced because of her wound. It was an effort for her to even speak.

"So Grimkahn will glide through the waters, taking out the largest shivers one by one," Grinder growled.

Silversun nodded, becoming thoughtful. "And the Seazarein doesn't know that formation fighting is useless against the horde. He'll need a new way to beat them."

"Let's focus on this battle first," Grinder said. He saw a scout tear back to his commander, who gave the mariners a signal to get ready. All snapped into attention hover.

"It's time," Kendra told them.

At least they had the current at their tails. That

would help a little. "I should get back to the diamond-head," Grinder told them. He had been chosen to lead the combined force.

The diamondhead was a position near the top and in the middle of a formation. Grinder's commands would be relayed by battle dolphins when the fight began. The mariners were well trained and their moves were second nature when in their own shiver formations. But AuzyAuzy, Hammer, and Vortex had mixed their sharks, putting them in levels; heavy sharkkind below for a base, the quicker ones above to ride the currents down. It had been done this way for thousands of years. But the sharks from each of the three shivers hadn't been in battle together; they hadn't trained as a whole. Even though their numbers were advantageous, this larger armada wasn't able to turn as fast or switch shape. It was a distinct draw-back against the horde.

Silversun blocked Grinder and Kendra and gave them a nervous grin. "I think I should take diamondhead."

"Are you crazy?" he asked.

Kendra nodded at the port jackson. "Silversun, we admire your courage, but ... but ... "

"Yes, I know. I'm not a fighter," he answered. "But you need to take all the mariners who are unhurt and swim away."

"Swim away? Never!" said Grinder.

13

"I know you think it's cowardly, but you have to save what's left of our mariners and get to Fathomir. Tell Gray what's happened. And figure out a way to beat Grimkahn."

Kendra straightened, gathering her ebbing strength. "It's a good idea, but I should do it."

Grinder shook his head and gnashed his teeth again and again. "No! Anyone who stays will be slaughtered."

"Then *everyone* will die for nothing!" Kendra said, slashing her tail through the water for emphasis.

"I'll do it," Silversun insisted. "I don't have the endurance to make the swim to Fathomir."

"In this condition, neither do I!" Kendra said, rolling to show her deep and ragged wound. Blood flowed freely from it. Kendra looked Silversun in the eye. "Maybe there's a way we could do this together."

Grinder felt tears welling in his eyes and whispered, "No, no, no . . ."

"Safe journey, old friend," the port jackson told him.

Grinder steadied himself. He wouldn't be a blubbering fool in front of the two. "Bite somebody for me, will you?"

"We will." Kendra nodded.

Grinder hesitated for a moment. It would be the last time he would see the Vortex and AuzyAuzy Shiver leaders. The last time he would see his friends. "You're the bravest sharks I've ever known," he told them.

Then, as Silversun and Kendra rushed Grimkahn and his horde, Grinder took the mariners that were able and drove them toward Fathomir as he wept.

Hokuu felt a thrill as he and the mariners sped toward the pitiful defenders. He couldn't believe it when Grimkahn had ordered the last attack stopped. Apparently the mosasaur king was still stung by his lack of victory during what the other side was calling the Battle of the Spine. Gray, that fat oaf of a pup, with a pitifully small group of sharkkind, had managed to find himself a strategic position on the Atlantis Spine where the current was shriekingly fast to buy time and had then used the Tuna Run and its millions of bluefin to pound the jurassics into defeat.

The pup was lucky.

Today Grimkahn wanted to see what the defenders would try next against the immense power of his horde. The mosasaur king was counting the days until he could eat the Seazarein's beating heart. That was a goal Hokuu and Grimkahn had in common.

Grimkahn, all the mosasaurs, and every frilled shark had been trapped in a pocket ocean for millions of years and, thanks to Hokuu, they were finally free. After their initial battle against Gray, their force had retreated to the Underwaters to regroup and train. Now they numbered a thousand frilled sharks and nearly a hundred mosasaurs. There used to be other jurassic dwellers: pliosaurs, elasmosaurs, plesiosaurs, and on and on. But these dwellers were impatient. They wanted to reap the benefits of the Big Blue without contributing to the fight. Grimkahn made the only logical decision and sent the troublemakers to the Sparkle Blue. He couldn't have dissension nipping at his massive tail, now could he?

The strengthened Sixth Shiver, the true name of the horde, destroyed everything that it faced. Now that he had reinforcements, Grimkahn wanted to devour every major shiver that might later ally with Gray.

And what a rush it was to fight with the jurassic horde!

The blood! The death! The shrieking cries of agony!

It was glorious!

Hokuu swam to the side of the main block formation. The very notion of jurassics lining up in a formation was revolutionary. Grimkahn had gotten the idea from facing Gray's forces and AuzyAuzy Shiver before that. Before this, jurassics had never even attempted formation fighting. They usually traveled and fought alone. If there were five of them together in a family pod, no group of fins in the Underwaters would dare attack them.

But here, sharkkind did fight them. And they did it in formation.

Puny and small though they were, the sharks of the Big Blue were also cunning and well trained.

They had inflicted unacceptable losses on Grimkahn's forces. So the mosasaur king had adopted a simple block shape. At first it didn't work. The mosasaurs were so big that the smaller mariners in the enemy formations could still get close and hurt them. Then the frilled sharks filled those gaps. It hadn't been Hokuu's idea, but he took credit as soon as it started working. With the ultraquick and agile frills to protect the mosasaurs, the horde, as the jurassic armada had taken to calling itself, became invincible.

They had even sent groups of fifty frills and five mosasaurs to other oceans. The objective of these so-called fifty-fives was to search out and destroy all the shivers they could find. They brought terror and confusion to every expanse of the Big Blue.

Hokuu adjusted his position so he could watch the initial clash from a safe distance. Then, once the opposing mariners tried to move a battle fin in their crumbling defense, he would blast those sharks with his shar-kata. Gathering power from the water was not as rewarding as sucking the life force from living things, but Hokuu couldn't do that in the confusion of a battle. That only worked when the subjects were still.

He could see the defenders clearly now. They came forward, straight ahead.

They were fewer than he expected. That was odd.

Wait, the sharkkind weren't all there!

Was it a trick?

Hokuu reached out with his senses.

A group of mariners had fled. Cowards!

Then he saw the leader of the defenders. It was a muck-sucking port jackson shark! He was struggling to keep up with his own armada! Hokuu laughed before the two sides clashed.

The horde ripped right through the defenders.

The idiotic port jackson was eaten in one gulp. Foolish fin! That would show him.

"No prisoners!" roared Grimkahn.

The blood in the water was thick and delicious.

A squadron of a hundred sharkkind led by an injured whitetip shark streaked from the side on a suicide mission to attack Grimkahn. She had the look of a leader, that one. With a flick of his tail Hokuu gathered a globe of sizzling energy and flung it. The orange power exploded in their midst, spreading through the water and electrocuting them all, including the whitetip.

Hokuu felt a thrill course up and down his spine. He loved battle.

The mosasaurs and frills made short work of everyone else.

"What a spectacle!" Hokuu shouted to Grimkahn.

The mosasaur smacked him backward thirty feet with his giant tail.

"You almost killed me with your foul power!" he yelled.

Hokuu couldn't believe it. "They were attacking you!" he replied in a voice louder than he intended. It was never good to yell at a king, no matter how wrong he happened to be. "I saved you!"

"Saved me?" Grimkahn chuckled, and it sounded like grinding rocks. "I don't need saving from these sad little fish."

"I was doing my duty," Hokuu insisted. "I'm not expecting any thanks."

"Of course not," Grimkahn said. "And it's you who owes me thanks."

Hokuu was genuinely puzzled. "For what?"

"You should thank me that I only tapped you with my tail," he answered. "Do that, will you?"

Hokuu's excitement about the slaughter was replaced with a bitter taste in the back of his throat. "Thank you," he said.

Grimkahn grunted and swam away to feed on the defeated sharks.

Hokuu's tail vibrated in fury as he watched him go. Grimkahn should have treated him with more respect. Much more. This wouldn't be forgotten. He needed the mosasaur because the jurassics from the Underwaters wouldn't follow him . . . yet.

Grimkhan was their king and Hokuu his first in Line.

But the day would come when Hokuu would be the one in charge.

Then Grimkhan would be the one doing the groveling.

THE OCEAN AT WAR

to hover. It was good for days like this. There used to be a hole in the throne for his tail but Gray's agitated swishing had broken off the top part weeks ago. "I'm okay. Maybe a little tired."

He motioned to Judijoan, the long and flat oarfish who was the keeper of all things regarding protocol. It was her job to keep his schedule, and the throne cavern in general, organized. Right now that meant making sure the quickfins gave their messages and then waited outside for any return orders.

Takiza fluttered his gauzy fins before Judijoan could call the next messenger. She paused as the betta fish spoke to Gray. "A wise leader knows when to rest." Gray ground his teeth. Lately, instead of insulting him in his usually flowery way, Takiza was being *sensitive*.

Gray didn't like this new Takiza. It made him tense. "A leader also can't swim away from his duties whenever he's hungry or tired," he told his teacher.

In the old days Takiza would have said something scalding in return if he had disagreed in the slightest. Gray had deliberately not said *wise* leader when he answered, offering the betta a chance to reply with something biting.

Takiza merely dipped his snout. "As you say."

Gray moved his tail back and forth in agitation. He wished he could go into the back caverns of Fathomir where he could be alone. Fathomir was far larger than he had initially thought when he swam inside the first time over a year ago. The caverns in the interior of the mountain went on and on and the place was a fortress. But Gray couldn't hide like a cavefish. He was the Seazarein Emprex and everyone was counting on him. "Who's next, Judijoan?"

The oarfish curled her tail and called a sleek and muscular blue shark forward.

"Message from Scarp, leader of Razorshell Shiver in the North Atlantis. Code word: Red Spire. The message is as follows. 'Seazarein Graynoldus, a group of jurassic marauders attacked our homewaters. There were at least fifty frilled sharks and five mosasaurs. We managed to send one mosasaur to the Sparkle Blue along with ten frills. Two of our battle fins were wiped out, and two more badly mauled. One remains in good order. The invaders continue north at a tenstroke pace.' That is the end of the message." The blue shark dipped his snout and went outside to wait.

Barkley sighed. "They lost over three hundred sharks and only killed eleven of Grimkahn's force."

"That's even worse than the reports from the AuzyAuzy and Indi Shiver battle," Leilani said. "Maybe Razorshell is poorly trained? They are new."

Judijoan shook the red plumes hanging from the crest on her head from side to side. "The news from Wannier and Puffin Shivers was similar."

"They're fighting better. They're learning," Gray

said, his heart sinking. He didn't allow himself to shout but he slammed his tail once against the remainder of the throne's backing, cracking it further. "Make sure our allies know which way the marauder force is headed. Also, send a quickfin to Salamanca. Maybe he can warn other shivers in danger."

Gray's good friend Snork the sawfish was with a giant blue marlin named Salamanca in the northern Atlantis near the Spain landmass. Salamanca was one of the leaders of the bladefish, a type of fin with absolute mastery of their bills, and Snork was his trainee.

Judijoan nodded. "I will see that it is done. The next fin seeking an audience isn't a quickfin. He's a shark on behalf of Trank the stonefish." Judijoan said this with a heaping dose of disdain. Trank was a poisonous stonefish. He ran a place not far from the borders of Fathomir called the Stingeroo Supper Club, where criminal activities were said to occur.

Although, to Trank's credit, the Stingeroo Supper Club served a delicious seasoned fish.

Much to everyone's dismay, Gray had met with the stonefish a week before in an attempt to gain support from him and his many questionable dweller friends. Most sharkkind didn't trust toxic dwellers. Gray didn't trust Trank either, but he didn't have the luxury of picking and choosing his allies. While Trank didn't have mariners like other shivers, he might be useful somehow in the battle against Grimkahn.

"I guess you'll get your answer now," Leilani said.

Judijoan sniffed but signaled for the shark to come in. Gray had heard from Shear, his captain of the guard, that Trank had begun putting sharks on his payroll. They were older sharkkind, most of whom were problem mariners let go from their own shivers: ones who didn't follow orders, things like that. So while it wasn't a surprise that a shark came to deliver the message, the specific shark who swam in was.

Barkley was first to recognize the battle-scarred hammerhead. "Ripper!" the dogfish gasped.

Gray had known Ripper for a long time. He had even called him a friend when they were members of Goblin Shiver, long ago. Of all of Goblin's Line, Ripper had been the strongest, the one with the most honor. That wasn't saying much though. Goblin and his shiver had done bad things. Ripper had been missing since the Battle of Riptide against the Black Wave armada. Gray thought he had been killed since so many sharkkind were never found in the aftermath of that chaos. Obviously the hammerhead had survived.

"Gray," Ripper grunted. "How's things?"

Judijoan shot a series of angry ripples through her long body. "You will address the Seazarein appropriately!"

Gray gave her a fin flick and the oarfish quieted. "It's okay. We go way back." He studied Ripper. The shark had a few more scars but still looked strong and capable. "I thought only old or crazy sharks worked with Trank."

"Who says I'm not crazy?"

Barkley shook his head. "We thought you were dead. How could you leave in the middle of the fight against Finnivus? And why didn't you come back for this war against Grimkahn? We could use you."

"Oh, I'm sure you'd *use* me, all right. Just like all the great leaders I swam with." Ripper laughed. "I fought for Goblin, fought for you, Kayless, Whip Tail, and half a dozen others who thought they were the ones who should boss everyone around. I'm done with fighting for kings and causes. I swim for myself now, doggie."

Barkley hated when anyone called him *doggie*, a slur for dogfish, but didn't press the matter. Ripper had changed. So had everyone.

Gray nodded. "Understood. So, what did Trank decide?"

"His answer is no," Ripper said without emotion. "No to fighting with you, no to allying secretly with you, no to helping you in any way. He and the urchin kings want to be left out of this."

Barkley asked, "Aren't you embarrassed about the sharks and dwellers that will swim out and fight for your freedom while you do nothing?"

"Not a bit," Ripper said, turning to leave. "For what it's worth, it's good seeing you two alive." Then he was gone.

Shear appeared above Gray and moved downward to speak. "I can wipe out Trank's poisonous nest in an hour. Give the word and it's done." The prehistore tiger was the commander of the Seazarein personal guardians. Since Gray was so preoccupied these days, he sometimes forgot that Shear was usually hovering over his dorsal fin.

Gray shook his head. "No. I won't do that. They have the right to choose. I won't force anyone to fight."

But in the back of his mind, Gray knew that soon, everyone would have to fight.

Or die.

CHAPTER 3

BARKLEY WATCHED AS VELENKA WENT INTO the golden greenie fields of Fathomir. The blacker-than-black mako with her big eyes and striking silhouette disappeared into the thick kelp. He had sent two of his best ghostfins, Sledge and Peen, into the area ten minutes before to set an ambush for her. Velenka was cunning, devious, and deadly. Her progress had been remarkable and she was one of the best ghostfins now. But while Barkley was beginning to respect Velenka's abilities, he could never think of her as a friend. She was much too untrustworthy.

And she had tried to send him to the Sparkle Blue more than once.

Now, though, she had changed.

The sulky and egotistical Velenka of old had been replaced by a shark who was eager to learn. She not only accepted challenges, but welcomed them. She had actually given a few of the newer recruits advice on how they could improve without being asked.

Not only that, but it was *good* advice.

Yes, Velenka was a different shark all right.

And Barkley didn't buy it for one second.

In the past all Velenka was ever interested in was power and how to get it for herself. If you were between her and that goal, look out. She even had the nerve to betray Hokuu! This caused the evil frilled shark to send assassin sharks after her. That was when Velenka's single-minded focus switched from gathering power to staying alive. It was a change Barkley understood.

But somewhere along the way Velenka had transformed yet again.

Was Barkley actually the cause?

He didn't like to think about it. For some reason it made him uncomfortable. During the Battle of the Spine, when Gray fought off Grimkahn and the jurassic horde, Barkley *accidentally* saved Velenka's life. A frilled shark had reared its ugly head to strike and in a moment of unthinking stupidity, Barkley rushed forward and shoved her out of the way.

That was when Velenka claimed she became this *new* shark.

She couldn't understand how Barkley, who loathed her, could do something so selfless. Neither could he for that matter. It would be one thing to save Gray or any of the sharks or dwellers he called friends—but to risk his life for Velenka?

That was a mystery.

And now he was stuck with her. She had completed ghostfin training in record time. The mako had been pestering him for more important tasks. Barkley said if she could stalk and "kill" two of his top ghostfins—by ramming instead of biting so there were no permanent injuries—then he would move her up to squad leader.

Barkley smiled. Velenka didn't have a chance.

Sledge and Peen, two hammerheads, were the best. And they had a ten minute head start to find a good place from which to strike in the thick, thick golden greenie. Barkley couldn't see anything at the moment, but he was sure the contest would be over soon.

Grinder and Striiker swam over, in mid-argument about something. Striiker was the large great white both Barkley and Gray had known since almost the first day they swam into the open ocean. He commanded the Riptide mariners at Fathomir.

"It's always been hammers on the bottom!" Striiker insisted.

"That was true one minute before I led my formation against the jurassic horde!" Grinder growled. "It was outdated ten seconds later!"

Barkley waggled his tail for them to be quiet.

"Guys, please. Go shout by the training field. I've got something going on here."

"We came to get your advice, so we gotta yell here, next to you," Striiker said. He and Barkley hadn't gotten along well when they were younger, but now they were fast friends and battle brothers.

Maybe we just grew up, Barkley thought.

"What *are* you doing?" asked Grinder as he looked over Barkley's head into the greenie field. "Watching kelp grow?"

Barkley snorted. "Velenka wants a promotion. If she tags Sledge and Peen she gets it."

"Not likely," Striiker said.

"How are my boys doing?" asked Grinder.

Barkley smiled. He had almost forgotten that Sledge and Peen, were originally from Hammer Shiver. "They both made squad leader a while ago," he told the hammerhead.

Barkley saw a glint of pride bloom in Grinder's eye. "I guess putting them with you was the right call."

"Yeah," Barkley answered. He thought he saw some disturbance in the kelp, but then it calmed. The current sometimes gusted. It could have been nothing. "So what could you two *armada leaders* possibly want to ask a dogfish?"

"You've studied the different armada stacks—you know about them, right?" asked Striiker.

"I know the theories behind the formations. But

34

you've seen me as a mariner," Barkley said. "It wasn't pretty."

Grinder gave him a tap on the flank. "That was before you invented a whole new type of superscout. Now we value your opinion."

"Fine, go on."

Striker did. "Hammerheads are heavy sharkkind that usually get stacked on the lower levels along with great whites and bulls. Grinder says we should put them somewhere else since they lost a couple times."

The hammerhead glowered at Striiker. "It wasn't just *losing*. They blasted through us like a swarm of krill. We gotta put our hammers somewhere else, someplace they'll matter."

"They're best on the bottom," Striiker said. "I've got a hundred thousand years of battle lore behind what I'm saying. If they were better on top or in the middle, we would know because someone would have done it already."

Grinder bumped Striiker. "If we leave them on the bottom, we'll lose. Guaranteed."

Striiker raised his voice "If we put them anywhere else, we swim the Sparkle Blue even faster!"

Then both sharks looked at Barkley.

"So, I'm supposed to decide between two losing strategies?" They nodded. "I pick neither."

"For the sake of this conversation, ya gotta pick one," the great white said.

Grinder flicked his tail. "Yeah, choose."

Barkley stared into the greenie. Something was definitely happening about a hundred yards to his left. "You need to think up something different. Something that has a chance of *winning*. Gray won't accept anything less and neither should you."

Striiker was about to argue but Grinder gave him a poke to the flank. "He's right. We're fighting about how to reorganize the levels in the stack. To win, we gotta think bigger."

The great white became more thoughtful. "Like a whole new type of armada? A whole new way of formation fighting?"

"Can it be done?" Grinder asked, in awe of the idea. "All those great mariner primes, generals, diamondhead leaders—they never did it."

Barkley looked at the two sharks. "But they didn't *have* to. They weren't fighting an armada made up of mosasaurs and frills."

"You've definitely given us something to think about," Striiker said.

The two sharks left, talking rapidly to one another.

Barkley turned to the kelp field and saw Sledge and Peen swimming toward him.

Neither was happy.

But behind them, Velenka was positively beaming. She looped around and around in a victory swim. "Who's the shark? I'm the shark! Who's the shark? Oh yeah, it's me!"

"Oh, come on!" Barkley muttered.

CHAPTER 4

SINCE THE DESTRUCTION OF THE COMBINED AuzyAuzy, Hammer, and Vortex armada, the horde swam wherever they pleased in the South Sific. The shiver Grimkahn was attacking today didn't even know how to get into a formation. They definitely weren't trained mariners. Their homewaters were beautiful, though. Complex and colorful brain coral grew everywhere, creating a stunning area teeming with dwellers and small fish. Food was abundant and predators few. These sharkkind had lived here for thousands of years. They probably never had a need to train.

Until today.

And now it was too late simply because Grimkahn and his jurassics were here and hungry.

The toughest of their mariners swam out to fight—if you could call it that—and were eaten. Others were so terrified by the sight of the giant mosasaurs, they turned and zoomed away screaming. But the frilled sharks had cut off any way to escape. Blood wafted onto the current in a pleasing way. A few minutes later the only sound in their homewaters was the satisfied munching of the victors devouring the vanquished.

Another shiver destroyed.

"HOKUU!" yelled Grimkahn as he ripped a flank from a large thresher shark. "Come here!"

"Yes, my king," Hokuu said, dipping his snout only a little. How he hated bowing before anyone. But he needed Grimkahn. The king had the absolute loyalty of the mosasaurs, and due to their many victories since they emerged from the Underwaters, he had earned the respect of the frilled sharks as well.

This made Hokuu angry. He was the one who made sure the frilled sharks were included in the new watery world order. But these frills knew Grimkahn as a king. They respected his power. And now he was giving them victory after victory.

But that current wouldn't last forever.

Once Grimkahn had conquered the Big Blue, Hokuu planned to take control. The mosasaur king would sadly die in a tragic accident and the jurassics would turn to Hokuu for leadership. All these thoughts flashed through Hokuu's head as Grimkhan made him wait like a fool as he stretched his massive, clawed flipper, digging it into the seabed and tearing up swaths of brain coral as he ate.

The mosasaur swallowed a smaller carcass whole and chewed thoroughly before speaking. "This is taking too much time. I grow tired of crushing these puny shivers. I want the Seazarein!"

"You made the decision to deny Gray allies by sending them to the Sparkle Blue, by way of your bellies," Hokuu said. "I know sharkkind aren't that tasty, but the plan is working."

"*Your* plan," Grimkahn said, eyeing Hokuu. "I wanted to swim to Fathomir and fight Gray. Or reduce it to rubble."

"Not even I have the power to do that," Hokuu said. "Fathomir is a strong point."

"No one is stronger than me!" Grimkahn yelled.

"Of course, my king," Hokuu said, dipping his snout once more. "But if we attack the fortress, Gray's allies can come at us from behind."

"So?"

Hokuu coughed, gathering his thoughts before trying to make the delicate point. *Because that would be stupid* was what he wanted to say. "Fighting in every direction at once, even with your new formation, has less chance of working than if we face them in open waters. He will come out, eventually."

"I don't want to wait for *eventually*!" Grimkahn pressed. "I want him now! Show me that I was wise to appoint you as my first in Line."

Hokuu nodded. The mosasaur had stumbled onto

a good point. It wouldn't do to let Gray pick the spot of their battle when it occurred. He had shown some small skill in the past at trickery, especially during the Battle of the Spine. "The Seazarein doesn't know where we're attacking next," Hokuu noted, thinking.

"Of course he doesn't know!" Grimkahn said. "As soon as you told me of those quickfins carrying messages back and forth, I tasked my fastest frilled sharks to eat any they saw leaving any area we entered. The Seazarein is blind!"

"Then maybe it is time for him to see a bit more."

Grimkahn swished his tail. "Go on."

"Gray is foolishly compassionate. He cares about fins he doesn't even know. The way to attack the pretender is through his soft heart," Hokuu said. He could feel his eyes glittering as everything came into focus. It was perfect!

Grimkahn understood. "I'll give him a chance to save someone. Someone sweet, innocent, and defenseless. Yes, this might work. You've earned your keep, Hokuu. For today. Now go."

Hokuu studied the mosasaur before leaving, bowing one more time. He was surprised the mosasaur king figured out what he meant so quickly. The king wasn't stupid. Rash sometimes, but definitely not stupid. Hokuu would have to remember that when it came time to kill him.

CHAPTER 5

"CONCENTRATE!" TAKIZA GRUMBLED. "YOUR mind wanders like a drunken sea cow!"

Gray didn't answer. He had learned over many, many training hours that most of the time Takiza didn't want one. Besides, shar-kata was hard enough without trying to carry on a conversation. And the betta did enough talking for both of them. "The power of the tides and currents do not merely wash past those who live in the oceans. Each fin and dweller is a part of it, their tail strokes and heartbeats add to the energy. Everyone is a part of this relationship. *You* are a part of it. . . ."

Gray let Takiza's words mix with the current and pretty soon didn't hear anything at all. Whenever he was free from his Seazarein duties, Takiza insisted on instructing him on how to increase his shar-kata powers. Unfortunately, there never seemed to be enough time. Trying to plan the attack against Grimkahn's forces took up much of Gray's day. Worse, it was mentally exhausting, so when they did get to train, he couldn't do very much.

He was all right at the first part, what Gray named *calling the sparkles*. He reached his mind out as if looking for sharks or dwellers in the area. Magnifying this, Gray could see the motes of power. There were millions and millions of them. More than anyone could count.

When these merged with Gray they gave him a boost of power. If he forced the matter, tried to will them to come, the sparkles stubbornly resisted. But if he relaxed and became one with them, they swooped over so fast it was hard to believe.

This Gray could do readily. He could gather power from the water.

He just couldn't use it very well.

"Good," said the betta. "Now swim the course."

He hesitated and Takiza cracked him with a gauzy fin on the snout. "Swim!"

Gray had speed-swum over to these training fields, not the ones in the Dark Blue by the Maw, but a different area in a less active section of the northern fire waters. What would have taken a week to travel normally took only a half hour using shar-kata. Gray was proud that he had been able to do this by himself.

But that had been a straight-line swim in clear waters.

Now he was being asked to go through an obstacle course a hundred miles long filled with razor-sharp coral spires. Shar-kata wasn't magic. If he didn't turn away from a thick coral formation or mountainside, he wouldn't go through it. Gray would splatter himself into it.

"I am still waiting," Takiza said. The betta had regained some of his previous sarcasm during their last few training sessions. It wasn't helping.

"Yes," Gray replied. "Your usual patient self, I see. Shiro—"

Crack! Takiza gave him another stinging snout slap.

"Oww!" Gray couldn't help yelping, but didn't lose the power he had gathered.

Takiza noticed. He had probably planned it. "Very good. See? You can concentrate! What do you want to ask?"

"I'm afraid I'll smash into one of those very solid coral pillars and kill myself."

"Then do not do that," the betta said, exasperated. "Begin!" Gray sighed. Just as he was thinking, Takiza would probably save me if I was going to hurt myself, his master added, "And don't expect me to guard you from your mistakes. I'm old and not as quick as I once was."

"The turns are so sharp," Gray said as he eyed the pylons. If he were to swim it at normal speed, there would be a good two or three tail strokes between each. More than enough time to adjust and angle his way through.

But using the speed of shar-kata . . .

Takiza tapped him on the snout again, but gently. The betta remained at ease and stuck like a barnacle on Gray's side through the entire training session, the better to critique Gray's every move. "Remember, turning is the same as swimming in a straight path."

"That makes no sense."

"No, it is so simple that you *believe* it to be complicated," Takiza said. "You can go straight with shar-kata, yes?"

"Yes," Gray answered.

"But your tail is not pushing you, even though you continue to wave it about as if calling for more seasoned fish. But it does nothing. That is why turning is the same as swimming a straight path."

Gray didn't want to continue the maddening conversation. The goal of this exercise was to teach him to move as Takiza and Hokuu did. They seemed to disappear, jittering left and right, and could stop on an urchin spine. For a shark without shar-kata to fight one that used it, a trip to the Sparkle Blue was almost always the end.

The last two times Gray had tried this exercise, he zoomed forward toward the first spire but had stopped to avoid crashing. He wasn't able to turn. This time he would get it right.

With a deep breath, Gray thought himself forward. Everything slowed down as if he was in battle, and he crossed the hundred yards of water in an eye blink.

. . . Turning is the same as swimming in a straight path . . .

It totally made sense!

What did it matter which direction he willed himself?

Straight, curved, zigzag—he could go anywhere he wanted!

Gray zoomed through the obstacle course. It was easy to zigzag his way through once he understood. He was moving with the speed of thought. What had been a cramped two or three tail stroke space to him before was a yawning chasm when Gray moved with his mind.

"Yes, yes!" he heard Takiza exclaim. "Turn around and do it again."

Gray whipped back and forth through the course ten times without a scratch. "Turning is the same as going straight, but in a curved way! Totally get it now. You're right, so simple!"

"Excellent." Takiza detached from Gray and gathered his own shar-kata energy. "Now, defend yourself! And remember, this is also the same, but in an entirely different way."

"Wait—what?"

Takiza released a ball of bright red energy and it hit Gray, stinging him so badly he thought he was on fire.

"Oww!" he yelled. "Let me get ready!"

"Hokuu will not wait for you to catch your breath," Takiza answered. The betta sped to the side and fired another bolt of energy.

Gray moved himself a good fifty feet and the next shot missed. "Ha!" he yelled triumphantly.

Takiza was behind him, though. There was a sizzling sensation as Gray got tagged again. "What?" the betta asked innocently. "I thought I heard you say something."

"Not fair!" Gray said as he zipped away, then back so he could face Takiza. The betta continued to hurl different types of energy. He threw bolts that boiled the water as they passed, ones that forked and spread like lightning, and others that exploded.

Gray put up a shield and blocked the attacks he couldn't avoid. Takiza nodded his approval, but after three hits by the betta the shield fell apart. Gray was jolted twice in quick succession.

It really hurt!

Gray gathered his own ball of energy and fired.

Miss.

"Again! Concentrate!" commanded Takiza.

They exchanged bolts, but Gray's weren't as strong as his master's. That wouldn't do, especially in a fight against Hokuu. He drew the sparkles inside him and thought about making them more powerful.

Then something happened.

The energy inside Gray multiplied many times until he felt like he would burst. His vision dimmed and he saw a different type of light. Not clean and white like the energy of the waters. This one was different, more like flashes and globs of color.

"NO! NO! NO!" yelled Takiza.

Gray fired and the betta dodged. The blistering energy blew a path through the thick coral forest. Once it was out of him, Gray's vision returned to normal and he didn't see the multi-colored lights.

"Wow!" Gray shouted. "Did you see that? How did I do that?"

"By almost killing yourself!" Takiza shook his head.

Gray stopped. "What? How?"

"You mixed you own life force with the energy of the oceans," the betta said. "Yes, it's powerful, but it can easily stop your heart. Did you notice the colored lights?

All of a sudden it hit Gray. "That's the Sparkle Blue."

Takiza nodded solemnly. "Correct."

"Great. I have Grimkahn and Hokuu after me and I almost do the job for them." Gray sighed. "I'm a jelly-headed, chowder-brained idiot."

"No," Takiza said, shaking his head. "You are the best student I have had in my long life. But that alone will not save you against a mosasaur. Though you cannot beat him without shar-kata, Gray, you must still keep in mind your limits. Until now you were physically the strongest in all the Big Blue and could solve problems by ramming them with your very thick head. That is no longer true. If you do not master shar-kata, I fear for the seven seas."

They trained for hours afterward. Gray's strikes got stronger and stronger and he avoided mixing his own life force with the energy of the tides. He was even able to launch attacks while he maintained a shield, for which he got another rare compliment.

But still, it didn't feel like he had enough power to beat Grimkahn. Or any mosasaur.

They were just too big and strong.

And then there was Hokuu, the most powerful shar-kata master the world had ever known.

When they were done, Gray's swim back to Fathomir was fast but depressing.

CHAPTER 6

THE SUN HAD DISAPPEARED BY THE TIME Gray returned to Fathomir. Though he had eaten a little—a haddock went directly into his mouth while speed swimming—he was still hungry. He decided to head into the golden greenie fields and hunt. It was a beautiful night, the water cool and crisp with a refreshing current whisking through the kelp. He didn't need shar-kata to catch five fat groupers in less than an hour and felt full for the first time in weeks.

For a moment, he hovered and enjoyed the silence.

Then something tickled his face in a familiar way. This wasn't shar-kata but a sense called the lateral line. For most sharks it was only a close-range detection alert, but then Gray wasn't like most sharkkind. Because of his training with Takiza, Gray's lateral line could detect the electrical shadows of larger fins up to a quarter mile away when conditions were right.

Even though he could not see a shark, Gray knew one was there because of the size of the shadow it cast. Or maybe it was a large bluefin tuna. Gray's stomach rumbled. He could go for a big bluefin about now. He swam silently through a copse of greenie and into a clearing.

Leilani was there.

The spinner didn't notice him. She was entranced by streams of glowing algae that floated through a valley in the distance. There was no moon and the currents were lit up by different-colored flows of algae. They moved and dipped with the waters, changing when they merged. Blue and yellow became green, red and green transformed to yellow, red and blue formed magenta.

It was beautiful and Gray sighed at the sight.

"Oh!" Leilani said when she heard. "You scared me."

"Sorry."

"It's gorgeous, isn't it?" she asked. Then the spinner shook her head. "I'm sorry. I shouldn't be so distracted by this dumb algae formation when so many are dying in the war."

Gray moved closer. "No, don't say that. If you can't enjoy things like this, then what's the point of fighting? Besides, you're right, it *is* beautiful."

"Did you want to be alone? I'm sure you have things on your mind," said the spinner. "I can go."

Gray laughed. "You were here first, Leilani. And no, I don't want to be alone. But I would like to *not* talk about Grimkahn, Hokuu, or jurassic hordes for a while."

"What would you like to talk about?"

"I don't know," Gray said. "You choose. Something you think is interesting."

Leilani thought. "Do you know how landsharks pick their leaders?"

They seemed pretty violent, so Gray guessed, "A fight to the death?"

"No, they *vote*," she told him. "They each choose their favorites and the human with the most votes is the leader. It's called an *election*. They elect their leader."

Gray laughed. "Really? What a waste of time! Wouldn't everyone vote for their friends?"

"Well, the humans who want to lead have to talk to all the different shivers in their home territory," Leilani said. She began to swim side to side as if she were teaching a class. Gray found this cute for some reason. "The landsharks of the different shivers listen to each one and then decide who has the better ideas on how to lead. Everyone gets one vote."

"What about royal votes?" Gray asked. "Are they worth more?"

"I heard it used to be that way, but now everyone's vote is the same."

Gray nodded approvingly. "And what if the winning leader does something totally different than he said he would before he was elected?" Gray asked. "Is there a fight to the death then?"

"I don't think they use mortal combat at all. I think they vote again after a time. You aren't appointed for life, only a few years. If they believe you're a liar, they choose someone else."

"And if that human dies, do they have a Line for someone to take over?" All shark shivers had a leader and what was called the Five in the Line. Number one would take over if the leader died or if the number one in the Line won a challenge. It had been that way since the time of Tyro, the First Fish.

Leilani nodded. "They do have something like that, but when the leader's term is over, he or she and their whole Line leave or have to be elected again."

"That's interesting," said Gray.

"I know," she agreed. "I was talking with Tydal, the minister prime of Indi Shiver, and he wondered if sharkkind could ever do it the landshark way."

This struck Gray as ridiculous, and he laughed out loud for a moment but then stopped.

Was the sharkkind way better?

Many shivers had the right of challenge. That usually meant someone like Silversun, a smart port jackson shark, could never become a leader. They weren't big and strong enough. But brains didn't always come with size. Barkley was proof of that. Sharkkind weren't really getting the *best* leaders their way. Mostly, they got the best fighters, some of whom happened to be smart.

"That would be something, all right," he told the spinner.

"We should get back," Leilani said. "Everyone is probably wondering where you are." Gray watched the masses of luminous algae drift and mix and change colors. It was soothing. "Another minute," he told her.

And together they watched the light show in silence.

They left a half hour later. Leilani had to go and check for quickfins from Jaunt or BenzoBenzo, her superior in the AuzyAuzy Eyes and Ears spyfish network. Gray knew that he probably had a bunch of urgent messages but there was one stop he had to make first. He felt bad taking time for himself but he wanted to do this. Gray veered toward the Riptide United's new homewaters, which were at the northern edge of Fathomir territory.

Riptide's previous homewaters in the Atlantis had been destroyed when Hokuu poisoned the waters so nothing could grow there. That was slowly getting better, but it would be years before anyone could live there again. There was a nice reef on the northern edge of Fathomir, and that was where he saw his mother, Sandy, a nurse shark. Though he was too young to remember, it was Sandy who first found Gray when he was a scared pup after his escape from the Underwaters.

"Hi Mom," he said and gave her an affectionate rub on the flank.

His mother ran her tail along his back like she'd done when he was little. It didn't really work anymore because Gray was too big for her to do this without swimming down his entire length. But it felt wonderful anyway. "It's good to see you, Gray," she said.

Onyx the blacktip gave him a hearty flank slap. He was an older fish, but cunning and smart. Barkley called him the original ghostfin. "Don't tell me Judijoan actually let you out of the royal cavern." They all laughed.

"I'm on my way there. I wanted to stop off before . . . " Gray trailed off.

He didn't know how to finish the sentence.

Before the world ended?

Was that what was going to happen?

Gray was so tired.

Despite a few moments of peace between battles, there had been crisis after crisis since Barkley and Gray swam out into the open waters from their home in Coral Shiver when they were pups. Would it ever end? "I just wanted to stop by and say hi."

"You look tired," Sandy said, her mouth barbels vibrating with emotion. She, of course, saw everything. Gray was her son, after all.

"Tired?" repeated Onyx. "You are mistaken, Sandy. The great Graynoldus, Seazarein Emprex, never gets tired, isn't that right, son?"

"Right," Gray answered. "I had a training session with Takiza. Those can be tough."

"See?" Onyx said, looking straight at Gray. "Not tired. *Recovering*. Big difference." Onyx knew that a leader had to be strong for his mariners and other shiver sharkkind. But there was concern in the blacktip's eyes. If the sharkkind fighting for Gray saw he was dispirited, they themselves might lose hope. He couldn't allow that.

"Gray! Gray! Gray!" said his little sister, Ebbie, as she tore over.

"Ebbie!" he exclaimed. "I was hoping you were around! Look how big you are!"

"I am totally *so big* now," she said, preening a little. "I think I'm big enough to swim into the open waters but Mom won't let me." Ebbie rubbed against him. "Can you tell her I'm big enough?"

"Yes, Gray," Sandy said with a smile. "Why don't you tell me that?"

"Because I've learned that Mom knows best!"

"Jelly-headed no longer!" said Onyx. "Thank Tyro!"

Gray used his tail to swish the current underneath Ebbie, and she floated to his eye level. "You'll have to convince Mom. I may be the Seazarein, but she's in charge of you."

"Aww!"

He looked around for Riprap, his little brother. "Now where's your—*oof*!" Gray was tapped with some force on his side—right on the liver, actually—by Riprap's version of a snout ram.

"Oww!" Riprap cried. "I think I broke my snout." Gray's brother was going to be large for a nurse shark, but he was still a pup. "That was supposed to hurt you more than me!"

Ebbie shook her head. "I said you couldn't paralyze him. Even with that thick head of yours."

"You didn't distract him enough!" yelled Riprap.

"So this was all a plan? How devious!" Gray said, acting surprised. In truth, his little brother and sister had ambushed him like this several times. It was all in fun. "Ebbie diverts my attention and you snout-bang my liver. Pretty good."

"Not good at all!" pouted Riprap. "You didn't even flinch! How are we going to send Grimkahn or Hokuu to the Sparkle Blue if we can't even ambush you when you're not looking?"

"We'll have to practice harder," Ebbie said in all seriousness. "Maybe we can get Takiza to train us like he did with Gray."

"Stop speaking foolishness!" Sandy said.

"Your Mum's right," Onyx said. "Let's go."

"Wait," Gray said. "What are you two talking about?"

Both Riprap and Ebbie came to the best attention hover they could. "We've decided to be mariners!" he said.

Ebbie added, "It's everyone's duty to fight in the armada. We can't be turtles, after all."

Gray exploded. "DON'T EVEN THINK THAT!" he yelled. Riprap and Ebbie were blown backward by the force of his words. "You're not anywhere near old enough to be mariners! Or even train!"

"Are too!" Riprap said before Ebbie gave him a tail poke to be quiet.

Gray wanted to yell again but saw his mother watching, calm as usual. She'd have an answer to this, so he motioned for her to speak. "It's true there are other younger sharks than Riprap and Ebbie training with the armada, but they won't be mariners until they mature," she told him. "Striiker wanted everyone to be familiar with formation fighting by the time they're old enough."

Onyx dipped his snout. "I've been helping with that. Didn't seem wrong, Seazarein, and no one gets hurt. Do you want us to stop?"

Gray thought it through. The mariners would be better prepared for the day they had to swim out into the battle waters. The knowledge would help them stay alive. It would be foolish to stop that.

But to train pups for war? What did that make Gray? He felt like a monster.

"Don't stop, but Riprap and Ebbie aren't allowed to join."

"*Whaaat?*" sputtered Ebbie. "That's totally unfair! You can't have one rule for everyone else and a different one for us!"

This was an excellent point. But Gray couldn't care less. His brother and sister would be protected.

"Oh, yes I can," he said, feeling a bit ashamed at his childish tone. "Because I'm the Seazarein."

"We thought you were cool, Gray," said Riprap, shaking his head in disappointment. "You're the worst big brother ever!"

Sandy gave Riprap a tap to the belly. "Say you're sorry this instant! Both of you."

There were grumbled apologies and they all had a group rub before Riprap and Ebbie went off to the rest area. Gray headed to the throne cavern, where a mountain of work was waiting for him. Mostly all he could think about was that Riprap and Ebbie were getting old enough to fight and fully expected to do so.

It is sad that all they know is war, Gray thought. They hardly even got to be pups.

SALAMANCA

CHAPTER 7

SNORK AND THE OTHER BLADEFISH WERE hidden in a series of greenie-covered caves off the coast of the Spain landmass. This was on the other side of the Atlantis Spine from where the Tuna Run happened and far from where Snork had made his home with Riptide Shiver. He had left Gray and the others to become a bladefish. His training had been hard, but Salamanca, his blue marlin master, had taught him well. And Snork was great at being a bladefish! He could now do things with his bill that he would have thought were impossible a few short months ago.

Tension tingled in his belly. He would need all of his new skills if he was going to survive the day. They had received word of a jurassic raiding party and set a trap. The frilled sharks and mosasaurs here were few in number, but powerful and ruthless. They had destroyed three shivers already, sending all their mariners and shiver sharkkind—even the pups—to the Sparkle Blue. Grimkahn had sent these marauders everywhere to cause confusion and destruction.

It was working.

Snork and the other bladefish had kept their snouts in the seabed for more than a day in the Galacia Shiver homewaters. Waiting was terrible. The Galacia shiver sharks were hiding, but their mariners, two and a half battle fins worth, kept a loose formation in the waters above.

The plan was for the Galacia mariners to engage the jurassics and then the bladefish squadron would attack from below. This wasn't Snork's first battle but it would be his first using his new skills. His stomach lurched and rumbled. It had been doing that a lot lately. Snork didn't want to let anyone down. What if he forgot everything he learned?

Stop thinking like that! he told himself.

The bladefish were a noble crew. Though there were only seventy here, it was still the largest group of the special fins in one place in over a hundred years. Bladefish fought for justice and tried not to take sides. They were a secret organization and didn't like attention. Well, most didn't. His master, Salamanca, kind of did.

One of the surprising things Snork discovered was that most bladefish weren't even sharkkind! They were *dwellers*: marlins, swordfish, spearfish, and sailfish.

Bladefish could be any fin or flipper with a bill. And it didn't matter if your bill was flat and edged, like his own, or pointy like Salamanca's. There were even narwhal whales with them. Those lived almost exclusively in the Arktik waters. One of the narwhals was quite a character indeed.

Aleeyoot was his name and he was an awesome sight. He was twenty feet long and mottled brown, black, and white with a shimmering green cast all over. His most striking feature was a nine-foot tusk coming out from what looked to be his forehead but was really his upper jaw. The tusk, or tooth, spiraled straight out and was made of ivory. It looked thin and delicate compared to Salamanca's sturdy bill, but Snork had seen the narwhal cut through a block of coral so dense it could have been rock.

Aleeyoot and Salamanca were the undisputed leaders of the bladefish. The only thing was that they didn't seem to like each other. In training they would go out of their way to correct each other's slightest mistakes. And they argued about everything!

Snork saw Salamanca waggle his bill to get his group's attention. The colorful lures in the bottom of his mouth clacked together softly. Salamanca told Snork that he had actually chosen the landshark lures that he wanted as decorations and hooked *himself* to steal them, breaking the line afterward to take his prize. The sharp hooks pierced the side of his mouth and were evenly spaced. Each hook had a colorful, foot-long lure hanging from it. One lure was of a glittering marlin, the second a row of colorful beads, and the third and newest, a carving of a curvy human wearing a skirt with a wreath on her head. Her hands moved back and forth with the current. "See? She dances for me!" Salamanca had told Snork before he took it. How did he even know the landshark was a *girl*?

Sometimes Snork wondered about Salamanca.

But not now . . .

The jurassics were coming.

There was a commotion above as the Galacia mariners got into their formation. Striiker would have yelled something fierce at those sharks. They weren't steady in their ranks and their pyramid formation listed to the left. At least the commander noticed and was trying to fix it.

The jurassics materialized out of the gloom.

They didn't even try for the element of surprise, the mosasaurs letting out screeching roars, eager for battle. The sound was terrifying, but the frilled sharks scared him even more. They moved through the water with an eel's grace and looked like a pup's bad dream. Though Snork had won a fight against a frill at the Battle of the Spine, he still had nightmares about the monster's mouthful of bristling, tri-pointed teeth and its spiked tail.

The square formation was bigger than Galacia's

even though the jurassics had far fewer fighters. The five mosasaurs were gigantic! How could sharkkind mariners hope to bite deep enough to do any real damage? That was why the bladefish were here. Hopefully their bills would succeed where shark's teeth had failed. They had to!

"Steady...hold..." said Salamanca in a low whisper.

The two armadas crashed into each other!

Within a fin flick sharkkind from Galacia Shiver began spiraling down, some bitten in half, others spiked through the head or gills.

It was horrible.

Salamanca took a deep breath and was about to order them to move when—

"ATTACK!" was shouted from their left by Aleeyoot.

That side of their hidden force sprang upward while the end Snork was on did nothing.

Salamanca shouted, "The fool! Go! Go!"

Snork and the right side of the hidden group shot toward the bellies of the mosasaurs and frills above them. Grimkahn's forces didn't think to look down. Maybe they didn't fear anything that swam in the Big Blue. Maybe they were overconfident. Snork and the rest caught up with Aleeyoot and the others before they reached the bottom of the jurassic formation and struck as one.

It was devastatingly effective.

Though the bladefish were few in number, they were all very skilled.

Snork was the least experienced out of everyone and he chopped a frilled shark in half with his bill. Yes, he had learned things: wonderful and terrible things. Snork wished he could use his bill only to enter contests with other bladefish to see who could cut fastest, or with the most precision. He loved those and actually won a few between training sessions.

But he was also trained to be deadly with his bill when needed.

And against the jurassics it was needed.

Bladefish had a code where they would not swim away from evil. They swam toward it, faced it, and sent it to the Sparkle Blue. The jurassics and frilled sharks had proven themselves evil. They could not be allowed to swim on.

The battle was chaos.

Snork's senses sharpened so that they seemed to scratch the inside his skull. He could hear everything: the screams of the dying, the ripping of flesh. He could smell the blood in the water, even the different taste of each species. The sharp vibrations caused by the frantic brawl pattered against his hide from all directions.

Something was behind him!

He knew it wasn't a fellow bladefish.

There was ill intent coming with it.

Snork acted on instinct and whirled.

He sliced diagonally through a frilled shark's head. The frill blinked the eye still attached to his head in surprise before Snork ended his life with a stroke through its neck.

Two of the mosasaurs lay on the seabed, unmoving. Another thrashed in agony, three of its fins cut off by bladefish bills. It was surely headed toward the Sparkle Blue.

Salamanca shouted as he chopped and stabbed his way through the frills between himself and another mosasaur. "Out of Salamanca's way! You are not a challenge. You!" he shouted at a mosasaur, pointing with his bill. "Ugly, large thing! Come! Salamanca would fight you!"

The mosasaur roared and flippered his bulk straight at Salamanca. The big blue marlin dodged its snapping jaws—once, twice, three times! Salamanca dove underneath the mosasaur and sliced the creature from throat to belly with his bill.

"Crude and slow, prehistore," Salamanca said to his dying opponent as he sank. "Your attack was no better than that of a clumsy pup."

But the marlin didn't notice that the last mosasaur was heading straight for him!

"LOOK OUT!" cried Snork.

Salamanca barely avoided the strike as the jurassic's jaws thundered together.

From out of nowhere, Aleeyoot drove his nine-foot

tusk straight through the mosasaur's eye. The beast stopped in the water, one of its clawed flippers jerking violently.

Then it was still.

Aleeyoot let the mosasaur slip from his tusk. "And that's three, my friend."

Salamanca bristled. "This did not count! Salamanca's life was no more in danger than if he were on a leisurely swim in the calmest of lagoons."

"Nyet! No! Nein!" disagreed Aleeyoot. "How many different ways do you want it said? You were chum and I saved you! Say it! Three times I've saved your life! Which is one more than you, who has only saved my life a puny two times. Say it!"

Salamanca sighed. "Three. But only because you swam off before my signal! You caused Salamanca distress and this led to a lack of concentration."

The narwhal crossed his tusk with Salamanca's bill. "If you weren't sleeping, I wouldn't have had to leave without you!" He smacked the marlin's bill with his horn and got deflected hard for his effort. They closed on each other.

"Salamanca grows tired of your overly big mouth and wishes to shut it."

"Maybe Salamanca should try that and see what happens," said Aleeyoot.

"Umm, hello?" interrupted Snork before the two began fighting. "We won. Isn't that what's important?

Maybe both of you great bladefish could concentrate on that?"

The two separated, both looking at Snork. Aleeyoot nodded. "Not a bad apprentice. Smarter than you, but that's not an overly large compliment." Aleeyoot swam off but before he left the area he yelled, "THREE!"

The marlin shook his head. "Salamanca is very annoyed, oh mighty Snork. Very annoyed, indeed." The big marlin gave him a wink. "But you are right. We did win." Then Salamanca waggled the lures in his mouth and said, "See? She dances for our victory."

CHAPTER 8

GRAY LEANED HIS FINS AGAINST THE THRONE in the Fathomir throne cavern as he listened to Grinder and Striiker. As usual Shear was above him and Takiza and Barkley floated at his side. He had kept this council meeting small. The two armada leaders were excited. They had been working on a new way of formation fighting against the jurassics and thought they might have an idea that could work.

Formation against formation, the mosasaurs and frilled sharks were too strong. A regular stack—heavier sharkkind on the bottom and faster ones on top—wasn't going to do the job. The jurassics were too big, the frills too agile.

What Striiker and Grinder proposed was to use each individual armada as a *battle fin*. That way the different armadas didn't have to be broken up and mixed, as was usually done. The sharks wouldn't have to swim beside mariners they didn't know. Instead, the mariners would stay with the sharks they had fought flank to flank with, fins they trusted. It was a huge plus.

"It's revolutionary, is what it is," said the hammerhead leader.

"Indeed," grunted Shear. "I haven't heard of anything like this and I know the whole of battle history to the time of Tyro."

"Not bad," Striiker said as he bumped the hammerhead. "You should take more credit."

Grinder waggled a fin at Barkley. "It was Barkley who got us thinking."

"I only made a suggestion," the dogfish answered.

"So your constant talking can actually be a plus?" Shear mused. "Who would have guessed?"

Gray flicked his tail to get everyone's attention. "I understand the advantages of when this super-armada breaks apart, sure. But what about before? If we swim out in a big, bulky pyramid formation with Hammer Shiver on top, won't that make us less maneuverable?"

Grinder nodded, "In theory yes, but the jurassics are slower than us. The frills turn well but have to stay with the mosasaurs, who can only move straight ahead in formation because they're slow and new to it."

Striiker agreed. "We don't want to engage them with our super-diamond. We want them to *think* that's what we'll do. Then each armada peels off, kind of like Indi Shiver used to do with their battle fins. That way we attack with a massed force at specific targets."

"So it won't be one on one," Shear said. "It would be the Riptide or Hammer armada hitting five mosasaurs, or a group of frills, all at once."

"Boy," Barkley said. "This sounds pretty good."

Grinder smiled, gnashing his teeth together. "We can make 'em bleed. But we'll still need another armada or two."

"Two's better," Striiker said. "Three, better still."

Takiza flicked his fins. "That would seem to be a large drawback as we don't have them."

The betta was right. Gray didn't have two or three armadas hidden in the back caverns of Fathomir. The forces that arrived with Grinder numbered seven hundred. Added to Riptide's ten battle fins, they were at seventeen hundred. They didn't know where Jaunt's AuzyAuzy sharks were, or if they were even still alive, so they couldn't be counted on. Either way, seventeen hundred wasn't enough against Grimkahn's main horde.

But Indi Shiver had a thousand more.

That would give them close to three thousand sharkkind when they added the new recruits in training.

Gray frowned. Grimkahn had a thousand frills and almost a hundred mosasaurs.

They needed more fins!

Who else could he call?

Hideg Shiver in the Arktik? Gray had solved a dispute between them and the orcas of Icingholme Shiver a while ago. Tik-Tun and his orcas would help, although Gray didn't know if they were migrating.

Judijoan poked her head into the meeting, her long oarfish body mostly outside. "I know you're busy, Seazarein, but you will want to hear this."

Gray nodded and Eugene Speedmeister came forward. The shiny flying fish snapped his four fins down in a salute. "Message from Tydal, minster prime of Indi Shiver. Code Word, Rose Spire. The message as is follows. 'The main jurassic horde is moving from the South Sific toward the Indi Ocean, destroying all shivers in their path. Both Grimkahn and Hokuu are with them. They are on a direct course toward Pax Shiver. Should we intercept?' That is the end of the message." Speedmeister saluted and left the throne cavern, passing Judijoan on the way out.

"Pax Shiver!" exclaimed Barkley. "The only shiver that's never trained mariners, never even been in a battle. Everyone leaves them alone so there's one place that warring sides can meet. Even Hokuu should be able to see the worth in that."

"I believe he does," Takiza said.

Gray thumped his tail against the broken back of the throne. "He's making a point."

Pax Shiver was named after a word that meant

peace in both the ancient landshark and sharkkind languages. There were over two thousand sharkkind and many more dwellers that lived there. And they were defenseless.

"It's a trap," Shear said. "They want you to fight on their terms."

"I won't hide while Pax Shiver is destroyed," Gray answered.

Striiker swam out in front of Gray. "Send a quick-fin and get the Indi mariners; we combine them with Riptide and Hammer-Vortex, and ka-bang! Right in the snout! We can win."

"Wait," Shear interrupted. "I do have to point out that you said you needed at least two more armadas. That's only one."

"It can work with one more," Striiker said, slashing his tail through the water. "I'd like to have time to practice but it can be done. Those Indi sharkkind are well trained."

"You fight with the mariners you have, not the mariners you wish you had," Grinder said.

If Gray didn't do this, Grimkahn and his jurassic horde would destroy Pax Shiver and then do the same to Indi Shiver. He wouldn't let defenseless sharkkind be eaten and he couldn't afford to lose Indi's thousand mariners.

Alone, each shiver was doomed. But together they might have a chance. The battle would be bloody beyond belief. It staggered Gray's mind that there would be such a huge loss of life, but there was no way to avoid it.

There was no other way but to meet them, snout to snout.

"Make your preparations," Gray told everyone. "We leave tonight." He looked at Judijoan quietly hovering in the back of the cavern. "I need to send a few messages." The oarfish went to gather the quickfins.

CHAPTER 9

TYDAL LET HIMSELF ENJOY THE PEACEFUL current flowing through the Floating Greenie Gardens in the heart of Indi Shiver's homewaters. He had been coming here more and more as the news from around the Big Blue had gotten worse and worse. Dweller master gardeners, mostly turtles and shellheads, made sure that the beautiful, flowering kelps were pruned to perfection. When certain coral lattices were closed, the current would push the flowers up and create a gorgeous pathway for him to swim above and admire.

Truly it was one of the wonders of the seven seas.

And it was doomed.

Grimkahn would destroy the gardens and everything else in the Indi homewaters.

"The royal families are gathered in the royal court," said Xander del Hav'aii, leader of the combined Indi and AuzyAuzy forces. The Indi armada was a thousand strong, but half were AuzyAuzy mariners Gray had ordered to remain at Indi after the war against their former leader, the mad Emperor Finnivus. Over the last few months, Xander and Tydal had become friends as they brought the mariners in their respective armadas together. The scalloped hammerhead had creases on his forehead that made him look as if he were constantly worried or thinking. These days Tydal had no doubt that Xander was worrying and thinking about a great many things.

"I suppose I can't put it off any longer," Tydal said.

"I reckon not," the hammerhead answered in his AuzyAuzy accent.

They made the short swim to the coral throne in the center of the Indi homewaters. Tydal had asked Xander his honest opinion about how defensible the Indi Shiver was. The answer was as Tydal feared: Indi's homewaters weren't secure. They had maintained their position in the Indi Ocean by not allowing any other shiver in the area to grow large enough to challenge them in the past. It had been a hundred years since the last real threat was obliterated. Indi Shiver had been secure in the knowledge that no one near them could match their mariners.

That wasn't the case with Grimkahn.

The mosasaur king and his jurassic horde could destroy them the same day they swam in. Tydal wasn't going to let that happen. He had to tell the other royal families his decision and it wouldn't be easy. Tydal would give the order to abandon the Indi Shiver homewaters.

The royals might revolt.

Tydal didn't blame them; he didn't like it either. But it was up to him to convince them.

That he, an epaulette shark, was leading an ancient royal shiver in the first place was extraordinary. Gray put him in charge and none of the royal clans had liked that. Tydal had to banish an entire royal family to put down their rebellion and it worked. The royals went back to bickering among themselves and that was good for him. But in this moment of crisis they had to pull together.

Could they put aside their differences? That was the question.

Tydal swam onto the rose-colored throne. When the sun shone above the chop-chop a certain way, it cast an impressive rainbow halo around the area. Not today. It was cloudy and grim, perfectly matching the mood of the gathered sharkkind and dwellers.

Oopret, his First Court Shark and another epaulette, got the audience to order. In a surprisingly strong voice he announced, "Minister Prime Tydal, the first of his name and title, ruler of Indi Shiver, will address you. Please listen first and there will be time for questions later."

Of course the royals didn't do this. They still

loved to flex their fins and poke at Tydal, though at least they weren't trying to actively kill him anymore. Representatives for the royal families shouted their questions and thoughts.

"I've been hearing of attacks against our scouts!" said a prince from Razor Tooth clan. "What are you doing about that?"

"Who is this Grimkahn?" shouted a princess, an older tiger shark from the Kaurava family. "Is he even real or did you make him up to scare us?"

"How come the mariners train so often?" asked a tiger from Taj. "Are you taking us to war without our approval?"

Oopret tried to regain control. That was the First Court Shark's job, but he was new to it. Tydal nodded to Xander, who bellowed, "IF YOU'D SHUT YER COD HOLES, MAYBE YOU'D GET SOME ANSWERS!"

This was highly ill-mannered, but it did get results. Xander and his mariners sometimes enforced a call for silence with a ram to the gills to quiet any who didn't stop speaking. It was remarkably persuasive. This time, no such action was needed, and the court grew quiet. The Indi throne was built so that the current would carry Tydal's words without his having to shout. Thank goodness for that because Tydal didn't think he *could* shout. His mouth felt dry, although he didn't know how that could be possible.

"You're all asking about the same thing: Grimkahn

and his jurassic horde. They are the reason the mariners have been training. They are heading this way to destroy us." Silence. Tydal had expected an uproar but everyone in the court was stunned. The leader of the Charavyuh, a more thoughtful shark than the others, waggled a fin to speak.

Tydal nodded to Oopret, who said, "The minister prime recognizes Sawtooth of clan Charavyuh." Sawtooth, who had been a battle fin leader for the Indi armada in his youth, asked, "Do you have a plan so that won't happen?"

Tydal leaned forward. "We can't guard the shiver sharks and fight Grimkahn at the same time. In fact, Seazarein Graynoldus tells me that alone we don't have a chance at all." This did get a reaction and there were panicked cries from some. Tydal raised his voice to settle everyone. "But there is a way. I've been in quickfin communication with Graynoldus and other shiver leaders. We will unite with the Seazarein's force. Everyone who can fight, no matter how old, is asked to rejoin the armada. We cannot leave a large group of defenseless sharkkind and dwellers without protection, so all shiver sharks must disperse from the Indi homewaters. The reason for this is that Grimkahn and Hokuu have been eating everyone they find." The rumbles grew louder and Tydal raised his voice to an undignified level. He didn't care.

"I understand that abandoning our homewaters

and going to war is not a great course of action," he shouted. "But it is the only option that I can see. I ask that the royal families support my decision whole-heartedly. If we do not swim together, we will surely be sent to the Sparkle Blue separately." The royals hovered silently, thinking about this. Tydal went on, "As a bonus, I will be leaving with the mariner force. Who knows, one of you might be king or queen within the week. But only if there's a shiver and homewaters left to rule. We must win this fight first."

Tydal settled back onto the throne. The royals spoke low among themselves. It was Sawtooth who swam forward. Tydal nodded for him to speak. "We didn't like you when you were chosen to rule by Seazarein Graynoldus. We liked it even less when the AuzyAuzy mariners were left here. But you've proven to be a good leader that doesn't play favorites. If it's a choice between you and certain death, we choose you."

Tydal chuckled. "So I win over certain death? It seems there's a first time for everything."

Though Tydal didn't plan on saying anything like it, the small joke worked wonders. The tension in the court released like a water bladder being burst. Soon he was laughing so hard there were tears in his eyes. And for the first time in a long time, Indi Shiver was united toward a common goal.

But now came the harder part . . .

Winning.

CHAPTER 10

VELENKA SWAM BY HERSELF BEHIND GRAY, Barkley, Leilani, Takiza, and the rest of the Seazarein's guardians. The ghostfins didn't bother to fast-swim or even move stealthily. It wouldn't matter in the numbers they were traveling. The entire ocean could see them coming.

She used to prefer swimming alone.

Now it wore on her.

Some time ago, maybe as she was being hunted by Hokuu's assassins, things had changed. The looks that she got, from those supposedly on her own side, made her feel bad. She wouldn't have cared before, but now it mattered. Velenka couldn't blame them. During the days-long swim toward the Pax Shiver homewaters, she had looked back on her life and decided that she had done some very questionable things.

Certainly she wouldn't be alive if she hadn't traveled the current that she did. Her upbringing was brutal even before her shiver was attacked and destroyed. There was no other way to survive but to be the best and most devious predator she could be.

That meant doing whatever was necessary.

But after Barkley saved her life so selflessly, remembering these past actions caused her great shame. Velenka had never, ever felt that before and hated it. She joined Riptide Shiver and the ghostfins with the goal of saving Barkley's life once and repaying her debt. Gray was no bloodthirsty ruler. If she asked to be let go after that, he and his friends would be happy to see her leave.

But Hokuu still wanted her dead so it was safer to stay.

That was the initial calculation.

But after a while Velenka discovered she *liked* being a ghostfin.

To be a part of this elite unit gave Velenka a feeling—it was hard for her to admit—of pride and belonging. This was especially true since she had bested Sledge and Peen in Barkley's test. Word had spread that she had beaten two of the best ghostfins. Though most in the unit didn't trust her completely, they *did* respect her. That was new.

Maybe it was something she had craved all along.

It was an odd time for Velenka.

The world seemed to be ending and she felt like a newborn pup.

Could she actually change the course of her life? Could she become a good and goodly fin? She had never given it a thought. Nice sharkkind were lunch in the Big Blue, and she prided herself on being ruthless. It was the only way.

But now? Now there was a chance for a brand new start.

Velenka worried that maybe it was too late for her to change. Or was it? Truly, these feelings were overwhelming. Could she toss away her old life and start over? Would any shark that knew of her past believe it? More than a few wanted her dead but she had to at least try. The evil course she had swum so far in life had brought nothing but enemies and pain.

Off to her side the massive armada moved along. Velenka didn't think it would be enough. She had heard there were a hundred mosasaurs, most fifty feet long. And there were a thousand frilled sharks with their ripping teeth and razor-sharp tails.

How could regular sharks hope to win against those beasts?

Still, Gray and his mariners went out to face them, snout-to-snout.

They fought to make the ocean safe for everyone in the Big Blue. Little sea dragons and tang fish that were too tiny to be a target of a frill or mosasaur didn't even realize they were being protected. It was illogical and foolish to risk your life for others who didn't even know you were doing it.

This sort of selflessness confused and humbled Velenka.

The tension in the water increased and she saw Gray giving orders to Striiker and Grinder. She followed Gray and his group into the Pax Shiver homewaters while the mariners in the armada slowed and bolstered their formation.

The current shifted and Velenka smelled blood in the water.

They were too late.

There were few corpses left, but the majority of those were only stubs of tails or heads. The Pax homewaters were devastated. Gray was staring down at something, his tail shaking with emotion. Velenka glided forward to see what it was.

She wished she hadn't.

It was a pup, a small girl whitetip.

Velenka's stomach lurched when she saw that the little shark had no tail.

"Why?" the pup asked Gray, her eyes wide. "Why did they do this?"

Gray had his mouth clamped shut so tight he drew his own blood with his dagger-like teeth. He couldn't speak.

"I want my mommy," the pup said, and then she swam the Sparkle Blue.

Then Gray howled, and it was terrible to hear.

GRIMKAHN STRIKES

CHAPTER 11

FOR A TIME THERE WAS ONLY A HISS IN Gray's ears. It was faint but drowned out every other sound in the ocean. His senses, so finely tuned, were dead. He saw nothing and smelled nothing. All he could feel was pain as he screamed into the water at the injustice of it all.

These sharkkind were peaceful and had done nothing to deserve this evil.

It didn't matter.

They were gone.

Seeing the little whitetip pup die had been the last thing Gray could bear. He felt a snap deep in his mind as the overwhelming weight of this horror came down onto his soul like an avalanche.

After a minute Gray felt the current buffeting him.

But it wasn't the water. It was Shear giving him a series of strong tail slaps to the face. Slowly, the others around him came into focus; Leilani and Barkley were closest.

"Stop it!" she yelled. "You're hurting him!"

"Enough, Shear!" added Barkley.

With a fin flick Takiza sent Shear spinning ten feet away. The betta told Gray, "You are needed as Seazarein. You must keep control."

Gray let the current streaming through his gills cleanse his mind. "I am here."

Shear joined them none the worse for wear, although he did give Takiza a look. "Scouts report that Grimkahn and half the jurassic horde are coming from the west. What are your orders?" Gray took a look. They were in luck. Grimkahn had divided his forces and there were only five hundred frilled sharks and fifty mosasaurs.

If you could call that luck.

But Gray was in no mood to avoid this battle.

In a quiet voice he said, "We fight. Tell Striiker and Grinder to get ready." Shear went to spread the word.

Barkley flicked his tail hesitantly. "Shouldn't we go to Indi first? Even though it's only half the horde we still need the mariners."

"Grimkahn is blocking the way and we can't risk circling around. They'd reach Indi homewaters before we did," Gray said. "If the ghostfins see a chance to take out Hokuu, do it."

The dogfish shouted, "Velenka, Sledge, Peen! To me!"

Leilani stayed at his side and Gray felt comforted by this. Shear rolled to his usual spot above Gray's dorsal. The ten prehistore finja were flanked above and below them. Gray swam past the armada as Striiker and Grinder got the mariners in order. The battle dolphs were in their places, ready to send the commands through the noise of battle. Gray struggled to remain calm and collected. If he let himself descend into a blind rage, it would hurt their cause.

He had to think!

Hokuu's amplified voice rolled to them with the current. "TODAY IS THE DAY YOU DIE, PRETENDER! YOU FAT, STUPID—" Grimkahn let loose with a shrieking roar that overwhelmed whatever else Hokuu was saying. The mosasaur seemed angry with the frill and snapped his tail at him as they came forward. Gray didn't give a broken clamshell about being insulted, but the way Hokuu's words drifted to them showed that the jurassics had the current with them.

Stupid! It was a trap.

Grimkahn had lured them from the Fathomir strongpoint and they were down current, no less! Striiker and Grinder quickly realized this and made adjustments. They moved their large hourglass formation—it was actually known as Triangles In, meaning the tops of the two triangles pointed at each other—to where the current was neutral. Grimkahn didn't understand how to use the water to his advantage.

He made no attempt to keep their angle, moving with Striiker and Grinder, and lost the current. Grimkahn led his horde straight at their forces.

The mosasaur king didn't need the current to win. With the monstrous size and strength of the mosasaurs and the speed of the frills, they only needed a solid hit and the Riptide United formation would break apart.

Takiza dipped his snout to Gray. "I would make myself useful in this fight."

"And I have an idea how you can, Takiza," he told the betta. "I'll draw Grimkahn away from the horde. You finish him while he's distracted with me."

"You would use yourself as bait?" asked the betta. Gray nodded. "I would."

"I don't like it," Shear muttered.

"We need to chop the head off this sea snake and it's worth my life to do it." Gray looked at Shear and his finja guardians. They had protected him without a word of complaint. "This will probably be a one-way swim so I release the guardians from their duty."

"Gray! No!" gasped Leilani.

Gray watched as the armada and the jurassic horde made their way toward each other. It wouldn't be long now. "It's my decision," he told everyone and then looked at Leilani. "You're not coming." The spinner opened her mouth to disagree and Gray slashed his tail through the water. "That's an order." He looked at Shear. "Take her with you. If I'm killed tell Striiker and Grinder. As for a new Seazarein, you're it, Takiza. That's for all the rocks you made me carry."

"A pox on you!" the betta said. He shook his frilly rainbow fins back and forth. "As your Shiro *I* order *you* not to die! Do not disappoint me, Graynoldus!" The betta zipped away.

"That's for the battle currents to decide," Gray said. "On your way, Shear. That's an order."

The guardian captain flicked his fins and went off, so mad he couldn't speak.

Gray swam toward the battle waters moments before the Riptide United armada and Grimkahn's horde were going to smash into each other.

But Striiker and Grinder were better than that.

The triangles forming the diamond formation split, one going high, the other low. This left Grimkahn and the strongest mosasaurs, located in the center of their formation, with nothing to fight. The mosasaur king screeched in anger and yelled, "COWARDS!"

We'll see who's a coward, thought Gray.

As Gray sped toward the battle, everything slowed down. To his eyes the Riptide United armada—now split into the Riptide and Hammer-Vortex forces—was swimming in slow motion. Striiker led Riptide over the top with his mariners, attacking the frilled sharks that turned. The mosasaurs in the center weren't fast enough to get into a better position so the frills were vulnerable. The frilled sharks instinctively formed a swarm but were too densely packed for their own good. Riptide attacked them ten to one, killing all they could.

On the bottom Grinder was doing the same. The mosasaurs pivoted, using their giant, clawed flippers to ride the current down to attack. This was easier than propelling themselves upward at the Riptide mariners. They had no plan and did it in a rage, so it was chaos as they rolled through the frills to get into the fight

"GRIMKAHHHN!" yelled Gray as he sped toward his enemy.

The mosasaur king turned in time to get a tail slap to the face. Gray slowed and turned a hundred yards away from the main fighting. He yelled again. "I'm here if you dare to meet me snout-to-snout. Or is it only defenseless pups you like fighting?"

Grimkahn was so surprised and angry at being tail slapped that he roared for longer than Gray would have thought possible. The very waters vibrated with his anger. Others from his force tried to join their king but he shoved them away with snapping jaws.

Grimkahn shouted, "STAY AWAY! HE'S MINE! HE'S MINE!"

The mosasaur king was seventy feet of white-hot rage, and coming straight for Gray.

CHAPTER 12

THOUGH IT MAY HAVE LOOKED LIKE IT AS HE hovered motionless, Gray wasn't suicidal. He planned on moving himself a hundred feet to the left as Grimkahn struck. That way he could counterattack from the side. What Gray hadn't counted on was Hokuu coming at him from behind.

But Gray felt a tingle from his early warning system, checked the electric shadow, and in a split second knew it was the frill attacking. It had to be Hokuu. Would he rip off Gray's tail with his teeth? Or use his spiked tail and go for the head? These questions couldn't be answered without turning and losing sight of Grimkahn. That seemed like a bad idea, and for a split second he did nothing. With the passing of that critical moment stuck in hover, Gray's choices became being eaten by Grimkahn or killed by Hokuu.

Or those would have been the options if it hadn't been for Takiza.

The betta zoomed between the two charging monsters and pushed Gray out of the way with a burst of power, leaving Takiza in position to take the brunt of Hokuu's attack.

Gray had guessed wrong. The frill didn't use his teeth or tail.

He *vomited*.

It was green and vile and shot from of Hokuu's mouth in a thick spray that didn't dissolve in the water.

But Takiza zipped away in a flash so most of the vomit attack hit *Grimkahn* flush in the head. The mosasaur roared in pain! He dove down and rubbed his face into the seabed, ripping up the moss and kelp there.

In all the confusion Hokuu had locked onto Gray as a target and hadn't seen Grimkahn coming from the opposite direction!

It was unbelievable!

The mosasaur had a look of thundering bewilderment on his face. He knew Hokuu had just sprayed him with something that was still sizzling on his face.

Gray could have never hoped for such a thing. How could anyone plan for something like, "And then after we get Hokuu to vomit acid into Grimkahn's face ... "

It was ridiculous to even consider.

But it had *just* happened!

Gray wasn't about to pass up taking advantage of this one-in-a-million occurrence. He amplified his voice and yelled, "THANKS, HOKUU! ONCE GRIMKAHN IS CHUM, WE'LL DIVIDE THE BIG BLUE BETWEEN THE TWO OF US!"

The mosasaur king's eyes hardened. He glided toward the frill, picking up speed.

"You cannot seriously believe that!" Hokuu shouted. "Do not do this, my king!" His voice cracked as he got more panicked. Then Hokuu made the mistake of gathering energy for a shar-kata strike. "I'm warning you!"

"YOU WARN ME?" Grimkahn roared. "About what? Your little hot flashes? Try them!"

Hokuu released a bolt of orange electrical energy with a tail whip. The forks hit Grimkahn but spread over his bumpy and ridge-like hide until they petered out. It didn't slow him down in the least! Grimkahn's skin seemed to reflect and deflect the force.

Mosasaurs were immune to shar-kata energy?

That was a definite cause for concern.

Grimkahn's jaws came together in a thunderous crash, missing Hokuu by an urchin spine.

"I'm your faithful servant!" cried Hokuu.

"Then serve me by dying alongside all my other enemies!" Grimkahn snapped at the thirty-foot frilled shark and took a two-foot chunk out of his lower midsection.

Hokuu shrieked in pain! He whirled and sent his

tail through the water with a metallic whine and deep into Grimkahn's cheek.

Now it was the mosasaur's turn to roar. He whipped his tremendous tail at Hokuu, who darted away and screamed, "You made me do that! I hope you die!"

And then Hokuu, streaming blood, swam away as fast as he could.

Grimkahn thrashed and rolled. "KILL EVERY-ONE!" he shouted.

Gray swam away while he had the chance. "Takiza?" he called.

There was no answer. Where was his master?

Gray looked at Riptide and the Sixth Shiver horde. It had been no more than a minute since the battle between their forces began. Riptide was doing well, but the size and bulk of the mosasaurs was turning the tide.

Striiker and Grinder were trying to withdraw but the frills and mosasaurs wouldn't let them. Then Gray saw another group of jurassics—the other half of the horde—coming from the side. Grimkahn had split his forces. Gray had been doubly tricked, it seemed. If the other half of the horde joined the fight, all their mariners would swim the Sparkle Blue.

Hokuu swam away, blood streaming from his injury.

All his plans were ruined because of a stupid mistake!

What could be worse than this?

Suddenly Hokuu had to dodge an attack by twenty sharks!

They were led by a dogfish—and Velenka!

"You!" he shouted.

"Yes, me!" she shouted, her eyes blazing. And Velenka came straight at him! The mako traitor succeeded in nipping his tail, and a flash of pain almost paralyzed Hokuu. Normally he could have disposed of this crew easily—it would have been fun—but he was injured. He struck at Velenka with his tail but only grazed her flank.

"Take him down!" cried the dogfish.

Hokuu tail spiked two mariners who came up from the seabed. It was lucky he had been twisting from the previous attack or he wouldn't have seen them and would have been struck right in his wounded belly. Hokuu moved fifty yards away with a burst of sharkata. Again, two hammerheads came at him from below as if they had been waiting there!

These were no ordinary sharks.

Hokuu gathered what power he had left and fast-swam out of there. He stopped a mile away from the raging battle, checking the seabed first this time, and then looking at his injury. It was deep. But with darkkata, Hokuu could heal himself good as new and gain the valuable power that he needed for revenge. He would need to steal life force.

A lot of it.

With a ripple of his wounded body, he moved himself forward.

This *hurt* and Hokuu's anger grew.

He would find his life force *donors* as soon as possible.

And after that he would see to Grimkahn, Takiza, Gray, and all the others.

Hokuu would see to them all!

CHAPTER 13

THEY WOULDN'T LAST MUCH LONGER, THOUGHT Striiker as he grit his teeth in frustration. His mariners were holding their shape beautifully. There wasn't a fin out of place. They were tearing through the frilled sharks in their path with a raking Topside Rip attack on the blocky jurassic formation. Even in the midst of the chaotic battle, he was so proud of them. With any luck Grinder's crew was doing the same amount of damage.

The problem was that the frilled sharks were too fast.

While splitting their mega-armada into two separate armadas had caught the jurassics by surprise, the frilled sharks were only confused for a second. After that they launched themselves upward and struck at the underside of Striiker's mariners.

Even without Grimkahn in the thick of it, they

couldn't win a snout-to-snout brawl. Striiker allowed himself the barest smile as he remembered Gray streaking past the mosasaur king and giving him the tail slap to end all tail slaps. It didn't injure Grimkahn, though.

No, it was better than that. It insulted the king in front of his mariners.

But Striiker couldn't think about that now. Dividing their armada had given them thirty seconds of relief with the mosasaurs stuck in the middle of the horde's own block formation. Now, the beasts were getting into the action both above and below. They emerged through the chaos. One snapped up two entire mariners off to Striiker's left, near his diamondhead position. The frills were lethal enough but the mosasaurs were too much. Striiker had to get his mariners away from this brawl.

"Seahorse Circles, down and to the right!" Olph the battle dolph clicked out the command as Striiker prodded his mariners. "Come on, we aren't here to see the sights! Move it! Move it! Move it!"

Riptide executed the maneuver flawlessly. Below them, Grinder heard and ordered the mirror image command so their two groups could re-form. Both Riptide and Hammer forces turned sharply, and the sides of their armadas fit together as they smashed into the side of the jurassic force. It was beautiful. Now the mosasaurs were jumbled and out of position at the top and bottom of their block formation. They could only watch as Riptide United tore into the frills in the middle of their formation.

"Long time no see!" yelled Grinder as they blasted the enemy in front of them. "Thought you were taking a break!"

In a one-on-one fight, a frilled shark would almost always win against even the largest mariner. But when there were twenty trained sharkkind mauling each frill at once, well, that was a jelly of a different color. Still, they would be eaten if they didn't withdraw.

"We gotta go!" Striiker told the hammerhead. "Let's break!"

Grinder gave a tail slash, meaning he understood. The hammerhead opened his mouth to give the command when disaster struck in the form of Grimkahn. The mosasaur burst into the battle and snapped his massive jaws onto the hammerhead leader.

Blood streamed from Grinder's mouth. He locked eyes with Striiker and gasped, "Don't give up," before being swallowed whole.

"NOOO!" shouted Striiker. He was devastated, but there was no time to grieve.

The other half of Grimkahn's force had arrived on the scene.

If they succeeded in joining the fight, Riptide United would be compacted and eaten alive.

"Attack!" Grimkahn roared. "Crush them!"

The other half of the jurassic horde roared straight at their tails.

There was nothing that Striiker could do to get his mariners away.

Gray saw that Striiker and Grinder had been preparing to swim away before the rest of the jurassics got into the fight. Grimkahn changed everything by killing Grinder and wading into the center of the melee. In the frenzy the subcommanders couldn't get Grinder's mariners ordered. And Grimkahn was big enough to occupy a hundred sharkkind by himself as he ripped and struck with clawed flippers, his huge tail, and crushing jaws. If the other half of the mosasaurs and frilled sharks enveloped their formation, none of the mariners would escape.

They needed a miracle.

And they got one.

"ATTAAACK!" cried Xander as he led the Indi-AuzyAuzy armada of one thousand mariners straight into the jurassics fighting with Striiker. The force with which they plowed into the mosasaurs and frilled sharks moved the horde's entire block formation a hundred yards to the side.

Most importantly, Striiker had space to maneuver. "TRIPLE TAIL TURNS UP—AND OVER!" he bellowed.

It was a risky move, but the Riptide mariners went over the top of the jurassic horde's block formation before the other part of the horde could smash them to paste. The mosasaurs had switched position from the middle to the top and bottom, then to the middle again. They screeched in dismay as Striiker and his mariners evaded them once more.

The jurassics and frilled sharks became confused.

They were taking much heavier losses than they were used to and being attacked by nearly three thousand sharkkind that weren't swimming away like everyone else. The horde didn't break but experienced a moment of panicked uncertainty when they fouled each other's movements. This small hesitation gave Striiker the seconds he needed to get the mariners together and out of there.

"SWIM ON!" Striiker yelled to Xander.

The hammerhead gave a fin signal to show he had heard. The Riptide United force—that's what it was now—streamed past the disorganized half of the jurassic horde they had just fought as the rest of Grimkhan's monsters got there, but it was too late.

But Grimkahn had only one thing on his mind—Gray. "You can swim, but you can't hide!" he yelled, battering his way from the melee and toward Gray. Gray waited and then moved himself with shar-kata as the monster struck. He could have swum away, but the longer he kept the mosasaur king busy, the more time Striiker and the others would have to flee.

Besides, now was the time to put all his training to use. Perhaps Hokuu had been faking when he attacked the mosasaur king. Gray would find out for sure. He gathered all the energy he could and fired a great bolt of power. It hit near the spot where Hokuu had injured Grimkahn with his tail strike but didn't do any more damage.

The mosasaur king wasn't even slowed. "That tickles!" he said.

Gray gathered power once more and released it with a *whoosh*. The bolt was strong—maybe not as powerful as Hokuu or Takiza's—but it had force.

And again, it did nothing to stop Grimkahn.

His heart sank.

Shar-kata energy didn't work against Grimkahn!

In fact, he probably couldn't hurt *any* of the mosasaurs using shar-kata.

This was a disaster. His practice with Takiza meant nothing.

And worse yet, Gray felt himself weakening from all he had done today. Striiker and the mariners were well on their way now. Gray swam away from his battle using the last of his energy.

Grimkahn yelled after him. "WE'RE COMING FOR YOU, SEAZAREIN! THERE'S NOWHERE TO HIDE!"

The mosasaur king had his scent and would come for the kill.

With some difficulty Gray caught up with Striiker and the rest of his friends using nothing but regular power. He tried to call the sparkles but failed and had to do it the old fashioned and very tiring way. By the time he got there, his head was spinning with fatigue. But he had no trouble finding them. Their formation was streaming so much blood that a noseless turtle could have tracked them.

Once he got there, Gray struggled with the twenty-five tail stroke per minute pace that Striiker had ordered.

They had to get to Fathomir. It was the only place where they wouldn't be overwhelmed.

"Fathomir," he said. He repeated it with each tail stroke until it sounded like nothing at all. "Fathomir, Fathomir, Fathomir ... "

The rest of his strength drained away.

Soon the armada was outpacing him.

"Fathomir, Fathomir, Fathomir ... "

Then everything got dark.

It seemed early for the sun to set.

"Fathomir, Fathomir, Fathomir ... "

What time was it? Gray didn't know.

"Fathomir, Fathomir, Fathomir ... "

CHAPTER 14

GRAY CAME TO HIS SENSES AND KNEW HE was moving—but he wasn't swimming. He looked around and saw he was jammed in with the injured mariners and being *pushed*. The cold current slapped him across the face and everything came rushing back. The clash between their armada and the jurassic horde, the death, Grimkahn's invulnerability to shar-kata, the memory of swimming away . . .

And then Gray had passed out!

Takiza, behind them and helping a group of injured mariners with his shar-kata power, saw he was awake. "You totally drained yourself. You may have even tapped into your life force again." The betta shook his head. "Haven't I told you never to overexert yourself?"

"No," Gray said as he freed himself from the bubble Takiza had created, which enclosed the wounded sharks so they could be pushed. Gray ached from the tip of his snout to the end of his tail. "You always tell me I don't put *enough* effort into your lessons."

"I will allow you the rudeness of disagreeing with me because you did passably well in the fight," the betta said.

"Oh, thank Tyro you're all right!" exclaimed Leilani when she saw Gray next to Takiza. The spinner shark brushed against his flank. "We were so worried."

Barkley broke off from swimming with the other ghostfins. "Good to see you up and around," his dog-fish friend said in an easy manner.

But Barkley also seemed *very* relieved.

Just how close was I to swimming the Sparkle Blue? Gray wondered.

"Hey, Gray!" yelled Striiker from his diamond-head position in the middle of the massive formation, which also included Tydal's Indi mariners. He gave Gray a quick fins up. "I knew you were only taking a nap! Now get back to work ordering us around!" The great white gave him a toothy grin.

Gray snorted. It was pretty funny.

"Where's Shear?" Gray asked. "Is he—"

"I'm here," the tiger finja said. The guardian commander and his finja were in their positions with Shear above his dorsal fin. Gray was really out of it and hadn't even noticed.

"You were guarding me while I was being pushed like a lumpfish by Takiza?"

"Yes," Shear answered. "For once you didn't complain. It was bliss."

Barkley snorted and then everyone laughed.

"If you are done amusing yourselves, perhaps you should formulate a plan of action," Takiza said. Gray noticed that there was a rip in one of his gauzy fins when he shook it back and forth in the annoyed way he often did. "We are being followed."

Gray threw off his weariness and the cloudy thinking that came with it. "Please tell me we're headed toward Fathomir."

Striiker joined them. "Sure thing. You kept saying it over and over before you took your nap." The great white looked deep into Gray's eyes. "You're not gonna do that again, right?"

"I'm all rested, Striiker," Gray said. "No need to worry."

"Please," the great white snorted, giving him a cracking slap to the belly. "Like I'd worry about you." But then he became serious. "Everyone else does, though. The mariners mope if you're not a hundred percent. It's super annoying."

"Shear!" Gray said, poking the tiger in the belly. "How close is Grimkahn? Are they all following?"

"Yes, he and the entire horde," Shear answered.

"What's our lead time?" Gray asked

"They would catch us in fifteen minutes if we stop dead in the water."

That wasn't enough time for Gray's taste. Not at all.

"I need to get a message to Fathomir," Gray said. "I'll be back."

"You will not!" Takiza exclaimed. "You must not exhaust yourself again so soon after losing consciousness. You could easily do it again on a shar-kata aided swim and kill yourself by smashing into something."

Shear, Barkley, Striiker, and even Leilani all volunteered to go. Shear reminded Gray that he was a prehistore finja with tremendous endurance. Barkley said he could fast-swim with his ghostfins. Leilani wanted to do it because she was a spinner and they were naturally fast. Striiker couldn't leave the armada but he had a few scouts that were race champions.

But Gray knew that none of them was the fastest.

He or Takiza were.

And he couldn't do it.

Gray looked to Takiza and noticed the betta was laboring. When he looked closer he saw that Takiza had more than one tear in his fins. When the betta moved to the side it revealed an ugly wound in his flank.

"What are you looking at?" Takiza asked crossly. "Now is not the time to stare with loving respect at your master. Actually, in your case, it is *never* that time."

"You're hurt," Gray said in wonder. He had seen Takiza do incredibly dangerous things and come away without a scratch. He also remained uninjured when Hokuu—who had trained him—tried to kill him again and again. But now ... "You're injured because of me."

"Nonsense!" Takiza huffed. "Do not blame your-self. It was not you who attacked me, was it?"

"No," Gray said, his eyes welling up. The thought of Takiza hurt made his heart heavy. "But I did hover there like a chowderhead so you had to shove me out of the way."

"Stop being ridiculous and deal with the problems we face!" Takiza commanded. "I believe the mariners that can swim faster should increase their pace."

Striiker nodded. "That's a great idea. We won't be bumping flanks getting into the Fathomir caverns like we would if we got there the same time." The great white swam off, yelling orders.

"Takiza," Gray said. "I need you to go ahead and make sure my mom and all the shiver sharks are inside. I'll take over here."

The betta shook his head. "You are too tired to use shar-kata to push the injured."

"And I won't," Gray said. "I'll swim with them. But I'm going to be the last one inside Fathomir. No one gets left behind."

After a moment Takiza nodded. "It will do me good to stretch my fins." And with that the betta dis-appeared in a stream of bubbles.

"ALL RIGHT EVERYONE!" Gray said, amplify-ing his voice. Even using this much energy felt like a weight was being pressed onto his heart. He couldn't do it for long. "I KNOW YOU'RE HURTING BUT WE HAVE TO GO FASTER! LET'S SWIM!"

The group sped up. A few of the injured shark-kind began bleeding more. They would have to push through it. Everyone would. Gray let himself fall into a deep concentration. He didn't want to dwell on how tired he was, or the danger behind them, so he focused on swimming and thinking of a plan to defeat Grimkahn and Hokuu.

And just where was Hokuu?

CHAPTER 15

ONE DAY LATER GRAY WAS SWIMMING mechanically, deep in concentration. The injured sharkkind had rallied so they were still with him. He was weary but could not rest even a moment. If Gray showed weakness, their entire effort would be wasted. He felt one of Shear's finja swim up and report to the tiger captain as they did from time to time.

"Seazarein, I would speak with you," Shear said in a low voice.

"I hear you," Gray answered.

"Half the frills, about five hundred, have separated from the horde and increased their pace. At their present rate they'll catch us within the hour if we do not speed up."

More than two-thirds of their forces had gone ahead to Fathomir but Gray's insides turned to ice. If the frills caught them, hundreds of sharkkind, including the wounded mariners, would be sent to the Sparkle Blue. But to go faster? Everyone was hurting so much already.

"Leilani!" Gray shouted.

"I'm here," she answered from behind. She had been swimming with him all this time and hadn't said a word.

"I need you to go ahead and tell Fathomir we're trailing frills," he said. "And make sure Striiker knows the situation before you leave." She gave him a quick bob of her snout and left. Gray hated when Leilani did that. She was his friend and it was too formal. "Shear, spread the word. Increase our speed to fifty strokes per minute. We have to win this race."

"I assume you won't leave the wounded for any reason."

"You assumed right," Gray answered. "I enter Fathomir last." The big tiger nodded. Soon Gray heard the change in the dolphins' pacing clicks. There was a groan from those swimming in the formation.

Striiker's voice boomed. "COME ON!" he roared. "YOU'RE NOT ON A LAZY REEF SWIM! MOVE YOUR TAILS!" Soon the mariners were a good quarter mile ahead. Gray didn't think this was a bad thing but did feel a twinge of regret that Striiker wouldn't be by his flank if there was a fight.

He would have to do it alone.

And Gray was tiring by the second. Exhaustion

descended on him with a vengeance. As much as he usually hated sitting on the Fathomir throne, he would have given anything for five minutes there right now. But there was no way he would leave his injured mariners to be eaten.

Absolutely none.

The enemy also sped up. He could hear the low thrumming their snaky tails made as they whipped back and forth through the water.

"They are fifty yards behind us," Shear commented.

"I know," Gray said. "Take the guardians and go."

Shear brushed against his dorsal. "I will not."

Gray didn't have the strength to argue and kept swimming. After their group crossed the Fathomir homewaters boundary, they were only minutes away, but it was still too far. A frilled shark broke free from the pack at their tails and struck at Gray but Shear rammed it away. Then two more joined it.

"We're not going to make it," Gray panted.

"You will," Shear said. "It's been an honor."

Gray was momentarily confused but then felt Shear's tail whip around as the tiger carved a turn and attacked the lead frills. Gray and the slowest of the wounded were given a twenty-yard lead because of this.

But Shear was gone.

Gray didn't notice Striiker sweep in with seven battle fins.

And neither did the frilled sharks locked in on their tails.

It was a destructive blow.

Striiker's force blasted the five hundred frills off to the side.

The great white hadn't left Gray. He had sped up to exchange his tired mariners for fresh ones that were already at Fathomir and turned around to fight.

Gray could have kissed the great white.

He pushed the wounded mariners into the cavern's main entrance.

Moments later Striiker and his mariners made it inside with the frilled sharks in hot pursuit. The frills could only try to force their way into the twisting main cavern entrance a few at a time though. That's what made Fathomir a strong point: a good current so sharkkind could breathe, combined with a defendable entrance to keep anything else out. The few enemy frills that breached their defense were quickly ripped apart.

Striiker hovered next to Gray when it was over, his gills flicking in and out as he caught his breath. He had surprised the frills so thoroughly with his bold attack that Riptide took no losses. "What?" he panted. "You didn't think I'd let you have all the fun, did you?" The great white flicked a fin above Gray's dorsal where Shear was usually stationed. "Where's your shadow?"

Gray shook his head sadly and Striiker understood that Shear wouldn't be joining them.

The great white's tail drooped. "Oh," he said.

"Am I interrupting?" asked a familiar voice. It was Tydal, the epaulette leader of Indi Shiver.

"Not at all," Striiker said. "I've got stuff to do." With that he bellowed at his exhausted mariners to get them in order. There was some grumbling but they did it. The great white had turned their fighting shark-kind into something special.

Tydal hovered in front of Gray, who remained on the rock floor. It wasn't the throne, but who cared? He was *tired*. Tydal avoided looking as if this embarrassed him. Then Gray saw that other sharkkind were watching with curious or even worried looks on their faces. Judijoan motioned for him to get up with her tail, staring death at him.

Gray heaved his bulk into hover. Apparently the Seazarein couldn't be *tired* either. "Sorry, had to scratch my belly and the lava rock is great for that," he said loudly for all to hear. This satisfied everyone and they went on with their business. Gray signaled to Judijoan that he wanted to speak with Tydal alone, and the oarfish nodded.

"I'm sorry I wasn't able to swim with you during the retreat to Fathomir," Tydal said. The epaulette looked at him sheepishly. "I'm not fast and it took everything I had to keep up with you and the wounded."

"The important thing is that you made it," Gray said. "Although we aren't in the clear by any means."

Tydal lowered his voice so no one else would hear. "So, it's as I feared. You don't have a brilliant plan to turn the current in our favor . . . as of yet."

"As of yet," Gray repeated. "I want you to attend my council meetings and help me figure one out." The Indi leader bobbed his head, accepting the offer. Gray lowered his voice so only the epaulette could hear. "Tydal, what am I going to do? I've trapped us here."

"As far as any mariner or shiver shark is concerned, I don't believe that's what happened today," the epaulette said.

"Really? Because I had a pretty good view."

Tydal smiled. "I saw a strategically brilliant maneuver that allowed us to escape a superior force. I saw a controlled retreat that got everyone to safety and frustrated Grimkahn and his horde yet again."

"Oh, come on—" Gray began, but Tydal cut him off with a tail slash.

"I, and everyone inside here, have confidence in you," the Indi leader continued. "And though we are confined for the moment, we are safe. That's the most important thing. The only thing." Tydal nodded and left, conferring with Xander about his mariners.

Gray felt better.

It was true. They were trapped.

But for now, it really was the best option available.

21

Barkley panted in a corner of the throne cavern. He and the ghostfins had managed to fast-swim one behind the other and beat the frilled sharks inside.

But it was close.

Velenka had also made it.

Barkley was unsure how he felt about that. She had performed well in the fight against Hokuu. But the evil frill wanted her dead and it was natural to take the chance and attack him. Once again Barkley questioned whether Velenka's new personality was real.

Was everything the mako did some sort of plot within a plot? He couldn't be sure.

Somehow Velenka knew what he was thinking and frowned. "You're worried that a traitor made it inside this cavern, aren't you? You're worried it's me."

"Don't be a crazyfish," Barkley said, keeping his face neutral at her amazingly accurate statement. "I'm enjoying not having to swim full bore."

But she wasn't about to let him off that easy. "If you think I'm a traitor then you should send me to the Sparkle Blue. It's the only logical current. You shouldn't take the chance you might be right. So what are you waiting for?"

Velenka bumped Barkley, who bumped her back.

"We don't execute fins because of a *suspicion*," he said. "But I'd be stupid not to keep my guard up given your past, wouldn't I?"

Velenka's black eyes blazed. But it wasn't with the evil intensity that Barkley had seen in the past. This was something different. It was as if she really cared what he thought of her.

And she seemed . . . *hurt*.

That couldn't be. Could it?

"I'm trying to change!" she said. "And I've done nothing to make you doubt me since I asked to join the ghostfins."

"Maybe you're waiting for the right moment to strike!" Barkley shouted. He lowered his voice. "I won't leave my tail unguarded with you. No way."

Velenka's own tail vibrated with emotion but then drooped. "I understand. Let me ask you one question, though. If I were anyone else, would you give me a chance to earn your trust?"

Barkley was struck by the question with an almost physical force. He realized she was right. When Ripper had come over to their side from Goblin's, Barkley was okay with it. He had even gone on a dangerous mission with the battle-scarred hammerhead. A few months earlier Ripper might have sent him to the Sparkle Blue for no reason at all.

The dejected mako turned to go but Barkley stopped her. "I'll tell you what Velenka. You make it through the next few days without betraying or killing anyone and I'll see what I can do about trusting you. Deal?"

"Deal." Velenka smiled a little before joining the defenders at the cavern entrance and making herself useful.

For now Barkley would hope for the best.

But he'd keep an eye on her, too.

THE
SIEGE

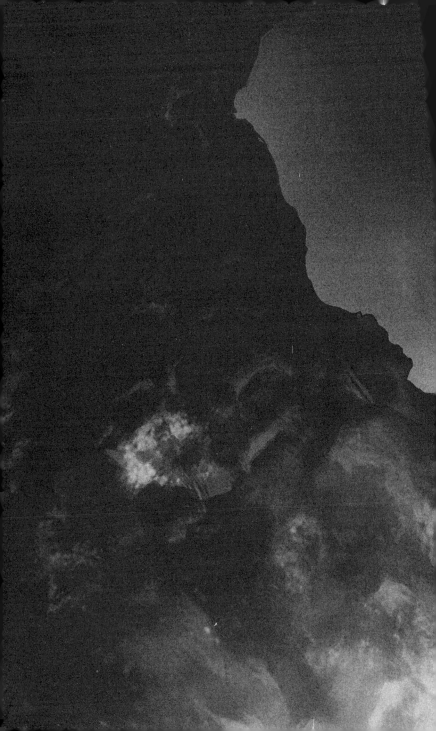

CHAPTER 16

"DON'T LET EVEN ONE INSIDE!" YELLED Striiker as he fought snout-to-snout with the frilled sharks pushing themselves into the cavern. The frills were a seething mass of death trying to jam their way inside. They ripped with their tri-tipped teeth and stabbed with their tails. If the armada hadn't been in a strong defensive position, Fathomir would have surely fallen.

It was their fourth attack of the day and the enemy showed no sign of giving up. But neither did Fathomir's brave defenders. There was only one main way in and out of the throne cavern for any dweller larger than a mackerel. It was suicide to do a frontal assault, but still Grimkahn's horde came. The mosasaur king knew that taking Fathomir was his path to winning the war.

One frilled shark writhed entirely inside the cavern

so he could move fully. The high-pitched whine of his tail spike whizzing through the water ended in a sickening *thwap!* as it pierced a mariner through the head. Thick blood bloomed in the water, clouding the cavern and making it difficult to see. Combined with the lumo light shining from the walls and pillars, it was an eerie and grisly sight.

Gray streaked forward and bit the frill's head off.

The horde was turned away once more.

Gray sighed, relieved. But he was taken completely by surprise when Grimkahn shot his jaws into the cavern. He scraped the rock walls on both sides of the twisty opening brutally but got far enough in to snap at Gray, who was bumped aside by Striiker.

Takiza released a bolt of energy, which may have stung Grimkahn, but as before did no real damage. It had become clear that his armored hide protected him and every other mosasaur against shar-kata attacks, and even the powerful burning vomit attack that Hokuu had tried. Grimkahn roared and pulled his snout out. Thankfully he and the other mosasaurs were too gigantic to get inside.

"You should be more careful!" Striiker said to Gray, irritated. "What are you even doing here? We got this!"

Gray was about to answer when Grimkahn roared from outside. "I KNOW YOU'RE IN THERE, PUP!" He went on in a somewhat quieter voice, "You're a cowardly little turtle, aren't you? Why don't you come out and face me? You did it once."

"Are these brilliant taunts working?" Takiza asked. The betta was in good spirits but looked paler than usual. His brilliant rainbow colors had dimmed. Or it might have been the light in the throne cavern. Gray hoped that was the case.

He gave Takiza a negative flick of his fins. "Even I'm not that chowderheaded."

Striiker yelled back, "Gray's busy, Yer Royal Ugliness. But me and my mariners are still hungry! Could ya send a few more frills this way? Because them's good eatin'!"

There was a cheer from the mariners after Striiker's remark. He really was a fine leader.

Riprap and Ebbie darted over. They thought the siege was a big adventure. They hadn't seen war from the front lines and didn't understand.

"What are you two doing here?" asked Gray. "Move back!"

"When you beat up Grimkahn, can Ebbie and I watch?" asked Riprap as he circled the group.

"Yeah, it'll be great to see you snout bang him good!" said Ebbie.

Gray shook his head. "No one is snout banging anyone for a while so you two calm down."

"Aww, come on, Gray, be cool. We know there's going to be a big battle!" insisted Riprap.

Ebbie nodded. "We may be smaller than the mariners but we can fight! We've been practicing on each other. I beat Riprap with Orca Bears Down today."

"Did not!" sulked Riprap. "Besides, I wasn't looking. And you promised you wouldn't tell!"

"If we need any help I'll come and get you," Striiker told the pair.

"Really?" said Riprap with his eyes wide.

"So cool!" added Ebbie.

Gray motioned for Judijoan, and also Leilani and Barkley behind her. "I need to have a strategy meeting and need some room." He looked at the packed throne cavern. With all their forces inside Fathomir, clear space was valuable indeed.

"I'll move a few fins around," Judijoan said, pausing to grace Riprap and Ebbie with a stern nod. "And you two stop bothering the Seazarein and go play." Gray's brother and sister went off as the oarfish continued, "Give me a minute and the space behind the throne will be clear." Judijoan moved off, rippling her long body and smacking sharks and dwellers that were too slow to swim out of her way. Even with a thousand sharks in the cave, her voice cut through the noise like a shard of volcanic glass. "Make way! Official business of the Seazarein Emprex! Clear the throne area or I'll have you thrown to the horde!"

A few minutes later there was space for Gray and his council to gather. Onyx, Striiker, Takiza, Barkley,

Leilani, Xander, and Tydal were there, as well as Gray's mother, Sandy. He looked at his gathered friends and family.

"There's no way to put seasoning on this rotten fish to make it taste better," Gray began. "We're trapped. So first off, how much food do we have?"

Onyx flicked his tail. "Not as much as we'd like, that's for bloody sure."

"We sent hunting parties out before we were trapped, but there are so many of us," Sandy told him. "We have enough to last us about two or three days."

"Make it three, then," Gray said. This wasn't good news. The mariners had been fighting. They used a tremendous amount of energy during battle and needed to eat. The longer a shark went without food the weaker he got. He looked at Striiker. "Are we really eating the frills?"

"Nah," the great white said, shaking his head. "I was only talking big. It's been tried, though. They taste terrible and made some of our fins sick. They might be poisonous."

"You got that right, mate," Xander said.

Striiker slashed his tail through the water. "Let them keep trying to get in. We'll take 'em out one by one until there are none left. Then we swim out and eat to our heart's content."

"That is not a solution," Takiza commented.

Gray nodded. "Takiza's right. And the longer we

stay in here, the more it feels like we're losing. If that feeling spreads to our sharkkind, it's over."

"But Gray," Leilani began. "Even if we could get out, how would you set the mariners in formation before the horde attacks? We swam inside here in a thin line. If we go out that way . . . "

"We'd be gobbled up one by one," Onyx said, finishing Leilani's thought.

"One problem at a time," Gray said. "We've have three days of food, so three days to find allies. I want the odds to be more in our favor. The only shiver large enough to help is Hideg Shiver in the Arktik and maybe the orcas at Icingholme. But to make it there and back before we starve? I don't know."

Everyone glanced at Takiza but Gray shook his head. "I need Takiza here in case Hokuu shows up. He and Grimkahn may have fought, but that doesn't mean they won't make up. And adding to our problems is the fact that shar-kata doesn't seem to damage Grimkahn."

"A definite drawback, I'd say," Xander commented.

"You didn't know this, Takiza?" Barkley asked. "You were in the Underwaters."

The betta ruffled his fins. "Yes, I was. But I was not attacking mosasaurs while there."

"Maybe you should have," Striiker said. Everyone looked at the great white. "I'm just saying."

"I hate to say this but what about asking Trank for

help again?" Shear asked. "What if we made it worth his while? Gave him territory or something?"

Gray thought about this. But the risk to the messenger was unacceptable. He wouldn't send anyone on a suicide mission.

Barkley gave him a tap to the flank. "I'll do it."

"*You?*" Striiker asked. "You hate him. And he doesn't like you much either."

"Yeah, but we have to try," Barkley answered. "And I can bring along someone who speaks his language."

Gray was shocked. His friend could mean only one shark. "You want to sneak past Grimkahn's frills and mosasaurs with Velenka in tow?"

"Velenka's very sneaky," Barkley said. "And she did want something more important to do."

Gray shook his head. "I know I've sent you into dangerous situations before, but that was when there was a chance. Trank already said he didn't want to help. It would be a wasted trip."

"Gray," Barkley pressed. "There's no choice. Unless you know where Yappy's secret, giant cousins are, we need to try." Gray let out an involuntary chuckle at this memory from their youth.

"He's right," Leilani told him.

Gray reluctantly nodded. They needed more allies.

Palink, the leader of Hideg Shiver, would come if he knew they were in trouble. So would Tik-Tun, who was king of the orcas. But how could they get word to them in time? Without shar-kata speed it was almost impossible to imagine.

Gray motioned for Judijoan and she glided over. "Do we have any quickfins?"

The oarfish paused, a sour look on her face. "Only one remained after the attack came." She motioned with the red plumes on her head. "Eugene!"

Eugene Speedmeister zipped in front of Gray, flicking his four wings downward. "Eugene Speedmeister reporting for duty, your lordship! What can I do for you, Seazarein Graynoldus?

Gray nodded. "How fast do you think you could make it to the Arktik, Speedmeister?"

Eugene flicked off another salute. "Faster than anyone, sir. And I like a challenge."

CHAPTER 17

SNORK WATCHED THE SCENE FROM THE greenie near Fathomir with a sick feeling. The frilled sharks were so thick they darkened the area in front of the main entrance of the throne cavern. They twisted and squirmed, constantly attacking, trying to force their way inside. A haze of blood obscured the entire area despite the current. And waiting behind the frills were the gigantic mosasaurs with their fearsome leader, Grimkahn, roaring orders.

Salamanca and the narwhal Aleeyoot looked at each other in dismay before signaling for Snork and the others to swim deeper into the cover of the golden greenie fields.

"Salamanca thinks we have a problem," said the huge marlin.

"Salamanca shouldn't speak in the third person

because it's annoying," said Aleeyoot. The narwhal was rewarded with a "harrumph" from the marlin.

Snork knew he shouldn't say anything with all the higher-ranking bladefish around but couldn't help it. His stomach was an ice ball of worry. "How are we going to help them? Did you see how many jurassics there are? And they're huge!"

Salamanca tapped Snork gently with his bill. "The size of your body is nothing, oh mighty Snork. It is the size of your heart that matters, and yours is very large indeed."

Aleeyoot moved his long tusk in short, agitated strokes. "But oh mighty Snork is right. There *are* too many for us. The Seazarein's mariners may all be in there. Safe for now, but how will they get out?"

"Obviously we bladefish will occupy the monsters so they can swim forth and fight with us," Salamanca said, irritated.

"Now's not the time for your particular brand of heroic stupidity," Aleeyoot said, making to poke the marlin in the flank. Salamanca blocked him, as Aleeyoot continued. "The only way we can occupy that force is to be sent to the Sparkle Blue by them. That still wouldn't give those good fins inside time enough to get out."

"Unlike my apprentice you obviously lack heart," Salamanca said as he tried to slap the narwhal on the head with his bill. He was deflected by Aleeyoot's ivory tusk.

"Guys, please!" Snork said, exasperated. "Can you save it for the jurassics?"

Both Salamanca and Aleeyoot backed off. "He's right," the narwhal said.

Salamanca saluted Snork with his bill. "It is not every day when Salamanca takes orders from a trainee."

Snork stared through the greenie at Fathomir. "We need to figure out a way to help."

"Maybe we can be a part of that," said a voice from below them.

It was Jaunt!

The small, muscular tiger shark gave them a knowing flick of her fins. "G'day. How're ya doing, Snork? Who are your mates?"

Salamanca grew irritated. "*Who* are *we*? Surely you jest. I am Salamanca and my slightly less skilled compatriot is Aleeyoot. We are bladefish extraordinaire."

Jaunt nodded. "Me mum used to tell stories 'bout you fins. Bladefish, eh? Good on ya."

Aleeyoot bobbed his long tusk gracefully. "Excuse my sometimes capable but puffed up friend. I hear from your accent you hail from AuzyAuzy Shiver. Did you by any chance travel here with friends?"

Jaunt nodded. "I did. Reckon there's about six hundred of us left. We split from the main force led by Kendra. She's gone." The tiger saddened for a moment but then stiffened her resolve. "Woulda been more of us but we were hit pretty hard by these krill-faced drongos twice on the way. We aim to get us some payback."

"Where are these friends of yours?" asked Salamanca. "They would be of more use a bit closer."

"Only if we want to be spotted," Jaunt said. "How many of you bladefish are here? Couple hundred?"

"There are about two hundred bladefish in all the oceans but only sixty-five are here," Aleeyoot said. "We lost five earlier. As it is, this is our largest gathering in many years. We do know that the Seazarein was able to join with Indi Shiver, so they are also inside."

Jaunt nodded. "Figured that. Then Xander's there, too."

"Let us attack!" said Salamanca, whipping his bill through the water. "We go now, correct?" Jaunt and Aleeyoot shook their heads. The blue marlin's tail dropped. "Salamanca's strength has never been in the planning stage."

Aleeyoot gave the marlin a playful shove. "Luckily we can put our heads together and think up something where you can be the big hero."

"Really?" the marlin asked. "Salamanca would very much enjoy that. I would also save your life twice more before this is over."

"Keep dreaming," said the narwhal.

"Maybe we don't have to come up with a plan," Snork said. "Maybe there already is one!"

"And why would that be?" asked Jaunt.

"Because Gray always has a plan!" Snork answered. "He's really good at that. Gray along with Barkley, Takiza, and others like Onyx, Leilani, Striiker, and Tydal. I'll bet they thought of some way of dealing with those monsters."

The group hovered in silence as they thought this over. "I have heard about Seazarein Graynoldus's great victories and I agree this is probably true. But how can our group be helpful if we don't know what they're doing?"

Suddenly there was a commotion.

It was different from the sounds of the frills attacking Fathomir. The group moved forward in the greenie so they could get a better look. Grimkahn's forces were swimming in every direction, shouting and smashing into each other.

"Are they . . . fighting?" asked Salamanca.

Jaunt moved forward to get a better view. "Well I'll be a squiddely kelpie. They're not fightin'. They're chasin'."

Snork saw a multicolored flash. "It's Eugene Speedmeister! He's a quickfin!"

The flying fish zoomed closer as he broke from the area by the Fathomir entrance. The group hid in the greenie until the fastest frilled sharks—in hot pursuit—angled off.

"We should help the brave messenger," Salamanca said.

141

"Got about as much a chance of catching that finner as swimming through a whorl current," said Jaunt.

Aleeyoot watched as the frilled sharks resumed attacking the main entrance. "If Graynoldus is smart, and it seems he is, he used that distraction to do something else. But what would that be?"

Snork thought about it. "There is one place we could check. One place he might send someone to make contact with us. It's called the Stingeroo Supper Club. It may be dangerous, though."

Salamanca nodded. "Then, we go to that place. Right? We bladefish live for danger!"

This time everyone nodded with the big marlin.

Jaunt took a last look in the direction where Speedmeister had vanished into the distance. "Sure do hope that messenger is a clever fin, or he's set to be lunch."

CHAPTER 18

EUGENE HAD LEFT MOST OF THE MONSTERS behind. The mosasaurs were huge but couldn't hope to lay a tooth or clawed flipper on him. No way. Eugene was proud he had caused such a massive disruption to Grimkahn's attack. It was just as the Seazarein had wanted. The second, much more important thing Gray ordered was for Eugene to get to Hideg and Icingholme Shivers in the Arktik and ask for their aid.

He would succeed.

The quickfins were being targeted by Grimkahn and his jurassics. Many of his friends had died carrying messages for the good and goodly fins of the ocean. He would, in his own way, make the horde pay for sending his friends to the Sparkle Blue. And he got to make the quicker-than-they-seemed frilled sharks miss him time and time again as he carved turns that even they couldn't match.

But not all frills were alike.

The two remaining snaky monsters chasing him were only twenty feet behind Eugene and keeping pace.

In fact, they were slowly gaining.

Could they keep it up for as long as he could? Probably not.

But they didn't have to if they caught him.

I'll have to switch from endurance mode to vortex mode, Eugene thought to himself through gritted teeth.

Endurance mode was what he used for longer swims, where his two sets of fins would stroke at different times, first one and then the other. Somehow it was less tiring. He could keep going for days, usually catching his food by swimming through minnow shoals or krill sieges.

He was still the fastest of the fast, quicker than a wahoo even, in endurance mode.

Vortex mode was a different matter. That way he beat both sets of fins, all four, at once. It produced more speed for a while but used up energy fast. And the current was against him. This affected smaller fish more than larger ones. A whale would swim right through a current that would push a small fish like him backward. The frilled sharks behind him plowed through the current while he struggled. Even with their odd, slithering way of swimming, they came forward easily.

Eugene knew that this was the reason for the illusion that frilled sharks were slow. How could they be fast when they sent huge ripples through their bodies in order to move? But that was where other fish who weren't experts in swimming like a quickfin messenger made their mistake. Though they looked like eels, a frilled shark's head didn't move back and forth, only their bodies. The heads, with all those ferocious teeth, came straight at him. Their bodies were like long, flat tailfins, and that propelled them through the water faster than most sharks.

Eugene heard the snap of jaws close behind. He estimated that the frill had missed by five feet. That was another advantage the frilled sharks had. They didn't have to reach his tail to attack like a shark would. By coiling themselves they could shoot forward six or eight feet depending on the size of the frill. It did cost them a little time, though.

Then there were their spiked tails. Eugene had dodged many on his way out of the Fathomir homewaters. He didn't want to do that again. That was the reason he wasn't in vortex mode already. Vortex mode was great for going in straight lines but not as good for carving extremely tight turns. And Eugene needed every bit of those fin-bending angles to get away.

His problem was the quarter of a second he needed to synchronize his two sets of fins into vortex mode. He had to start both sets together. Normally this wasn't an issue. Gliding for a quarter second was no big deal. The majority of dwellers in the ocean couldn't even tell when Eugene did it.

But right now, fouling his own stroke pattern for a quarter second, the frills would catch him. And to switch over with the current in his face, Eugene would lose a lot of speed, maybe even be pushed to a complete stop for a fin flick.

SNAP!

One of the frilled sharks tried to eat him again.

They were gaining. Only three feet behind now.

The head-on current was allowing the frills to creep ever closer.

These had to be the fastest frills in the world.

Suddenly Eugene got a bad feeling and swung left.

It was a good thing he did.

A frilled shark smashed his jaws together right where he had been swimming.

They were on him!

There was no way Eugene could safely give up that quarter second.

There was only one thing to do.

It was risky, dangerous, and extreme.

But that's what I'm all about, thought Eugene. I am the Speedmeister, the fastest of the fast, the quickest of the quickfins, and these lumpfish won't keep me from delivering my duly appointed message!

Eugene streaked straight up toward the chop-chop.

The move caught the frilled sharks by surprise and they shot past him by twenty feet. If Eugene had been in vortex mode he never could have angled so sharply. The frilled sharks corrected, lightning fast. He tore through the water, up-up-up!

The light of the sun grew so bright it was blinding. Still he climbed, pushing himself faster and faster. He would need every ounce of his strength.

With one final push Eugene burst through the chop-chop and into the air.

He heard the snap of frill teeth but they missed.

Eugene soared into the air. For a moment it seemed he could fly like a seabird.

But, and he knew this well, he wasn't a seabird.

No, in Eugene's case, what went up would definitely come down . . .

Straight into a frilled shark's hungry maw.

His gills slapped shut. He wasn't a bird after all and couldn't breathe air. But he could hold his breath while above the water. He was great at it, actually. And his fins allowed him to glide when he caught the wind. Eugene's paddle tail could push his body back above the chop-chop time and time again, keeping himself aloft for as long as the wind currents were right. It was dangerous to launch yourself into the air without knowing which way the wind above was blowing. Usually it moved with the current, but sometimes not.

To glide, Eugene needed the wind to be against him.

He also needed to synchronize his fins into glide mode. This took as long as getting into vortex mode but was slightly different, of course. Eugene would beat his two sets of fins in whatever order caught the wind best. Glide mode was the toughest one to learn. Sometimes you needed to jump more than once into the air. First to tell which way the wind was blowing and how hard, then to give yourself the angle you needed to glide.

You didn't launch yourself up without knowing this because if you didn't get your glide going, you would crash into the water. That could really hurt.

In this case it wouldn't hurt.

He would be eaten in one gulp.

Eugene fell.

As his body turned he saw the frilled sharks jostling for position. They were both panting heavily and wanted the prize of eating him.

Eugene spread his fins, shaking the water off them with a hard flap.

His first attempt to get into glide mode was ruined by a gust of wind which spun him around.

He spiraled toward the mouth of one of the frilled sharks.

I will not fail! he yelled at himself.

SWAP-SWAP! His fins caught the wind on his second attempt.

Eugene zoomed over both frilled sharks, yelling to them as he passed, "I AM THE SPEEDMEISTER! EAT MY *WAAAAAKE*!"

It was three minutes before he skimmed back into the water. He had glided over a mile above the chop-chop, a personal best.

It was still going to be a long swim, but Eugene didn't mind one bit.

CHAPTER 19

HOKUU WRITHED IN PAIN AS THE SHARKKIND of Jetty Shiver gathered before him. He was feverish from Grimkahn's bite as well as the smaller wound from Velenka. Jetty's homewaters were over a stunning black coral reef made up of tens of thousands of delicate fans that seemed to wave at Hokuu, wishing him good luck.

I don't need luck, he thought, smelling his own blood in the water.

The Jetty Shiver fools had attacked him earlier. Now he would teach them a lesson. Their leader was a young thresher shark named Conton. "We're all here, like you asked," he said. "Please, give your speech and then go in peace."

Hokuu nodded. Even that effort caused his wound to stretch and hurt like fire. He had found the hidden shiver numbering a thousand sharkkind by sheer luck when his fever spiked and he wandered into their territory. Hokuu still didn't know anyone was there until they attacked. After Hokuu killed twenty or so of their sharks, the leader decided it was time to talk.

Hokuu told them he was a prophet and all he wanted to do was preach the word of the coming future. Conton and his Line were so relieved there wouldn't be any more fighting, they immediately agreed. The thresher leader was young and in over his head.

"Good," Hokuu told the thresher. "As I said, all I want to do is enlighten you. I only wish I hadn't been so viciously attacked."

Conton flicked his tail nervously. "I said I was sorry for that. But you didn't stop the five times the guards asked you to. They had to think about the safety of the shiver."

"So you attacked a poor, wounded prophet," Hokuu said, swishing his tail as he gathered the dark-kata power. It hurt so much his head swam and his vision got blurry, but it had to be done or he would die. "You and Jetty Shiver should be so proud."

Conton mumbled "sorry" once more.

Hokuu had drained the life force of a few groups of fish and sharkkind after he fled Grimkahn, but it wasn't enough. And shar-kata was useless for this type of injury. The only way to heal was a massive infusion of power that only dark-kata would bring.

"I need everyone to look at me!" Hokuu announced. "Look at my tail. See how it circles? So circle the waters of the seven seas, moving from one ocean to the other in an endless current." Whether or not this was true, Hokuu didn't care. Getting the shiver shark-kind to watch the pulsing greenness of his dark-kata spell was the point. The hypnotic power that would steal their lives also gave him control of their bodies so they couldn't flee.

The energy grew brighter and brighter.

Hokuu extended tendrils from the center of the dark-kata vortex with his own life force and sent these through the packed homewaters. These force lines connected each and every sharkkind and dweller that was watching to him.

Hokuu could feel a few frightened Jetty sharks try to turn or avert their eyes.

But they couldn't.

He had them.

It was so easy. He was about to send an entire shiver to the Sparkle Blue and it had been pup's play.

That thought should have brought a smile to Hokuu's face, but it didn't.

His well-laid plans had been ruined once again. Sometimes it seemed the ocean itself was against him. It was so frustrating! He had been doing everything right and that fat pup managed to turn his current of victory into defeat once more!

How could Grimkahn have believed Gray?

"Why did you stop?" asked Conton. "Hey! I—I can't move! What's happening?"

"Shut up," Hokuu told the thresher. "I'm thinking."

Of course Hokuu *was* going to betray Grimkahn.

But that would be later, when the Big Blue was securely in the mosasaur king's clawed flippers and Hokuu could mysteriously kill him. After a respectful funeral ceremony, he would have been in perfect position to swim from first in Line to being the new ruler of the Big Blue.

Now that wouldn't happen.

It was all Gray's fault.

Grimkahn would be punished for his stupidity and causing Hokuu pain.

But Gray?

Hokuu would eat Gray, mouthful by mouthful, from the tail up. And he would use his power to keep the pretender alive as he did it.

Takiza was too small to be a meal, so maybe he'd be a light dessert.

But first things first. . . .

Hokuu looked out over the paralyzed crowd. Some Jetty sharks had been pushed into awkward positions by the current as he had been pondering his situation. That was all right. They wouldn't be uncomfortable too much longer.

"I have something to say," Hokuu said. "It's about

knowing your place. Any given day in the Big Blue you can have lunch, or be lunch. Today, you're my lunch." Hokuu could see their shock and terror, and it warmed him. There were a few muffled grunts from the stronger sharkkind but nothing more since he had paralyzed their throats.

He didn't want to be interrupted, especially during his brilliant speech.

Hokuu reversed the flow of the dark-kata, dragging the life force energy from each shark and dweller from Jetty Shiver to his own body.

The weakest among them, the old and young, died in a wave.

"When you woke up today you fully expected to have lunch, not be lunch. You didn't *really* know your place. That's how it is with everyone else in the Big Blue. No one understands that I am the greatest fin that has ever swum the waters, greater than Tyro even!"

Hokuu's voice rose as dark-kata energy filled him to bursting. It was wonderful! It was glorious! He felt his wound close up and heal. Still he sucked at their life force greedily, making sure to take every last bit. There was a collective moan from those still alive as they felt themselves dying. Hokuu's power grew until he glowed, shining bright as if he had swallowed a piece of a wicked, green sun.

"Like the others, you didn't realize that I am your

king! You should have driven your snouts into the muck when you saw me. The Seazarein doesn't understand either, but he will! Oh, how he will! I swear that like you, everyone will know this fact by the time I am done!"

Hokuu surveyed the silent scene in front of him.

Every sharkkind and dweller—even the polyps that were responsible for the beautiful black coral fans—was gray and dead. The current carried away the flakes, which crumbled from everything affected by his spell. Hokuu had seen snow falling into the ocean a few times. This looked like that, but in reverse, as the flakes floated up and away from the Jetty Shiver homewaters.

It was pretty in a way, and this pleased Hokuu. It was a vision of the future for Gray and his friends, for Grimkahn, and for the rest of his jurassics.

Everyone would get what was coming to them. Hokuu would see to it.

With a snap of his spiked tail he turned the corpse of Conton into a cloud of floating gray and white flakes. Hokuu swam through the quiet crowd. The sharkkind and dwellers of Jetty Shiver seemed to be watching him, their black eye holes watching—maybe judging—as he swam toward his destiny.

Let them stare, thought Hokuu. They're all jealous.

And with every swish of his tail, Hokuu sent blooms of ash upward into the water.

CHAPTER 20

GRAY DISMISSED THE REST OF HIS ADVISORS after they had gone over the events of the day. Only Takiza was left in the small private chamber. Gray had to order the betta to allow himself to be examined by Oceania, a surgeonfish. The white lumo light in this particular cavern cast everything in a ghostly half-light that Gray found unsettling.

"Will you stop your infernal prodding?" Takiza huffed. "The wound is tender. You are not aiding matters by poking it!"

"Hold still," Oceania said, ignoring the betta.

Speedmeister was on his way to the Arktik. Gray hoped the resourceful little fish would find a way to get there. But could Hideg and Icingholme Shivers even swim from the north to Fathomir in time?

Barkley and Velenka had also managed to slip out during Speedmeister's mad swim. Gray worried that he had sent his best friend on a fool's errand to convince Trank. The stonefish might even decide that capturing Barkley and Velenka and giving them to Grimkahn would be a better idea. And then, of course, there was the continuing threat of the jurassic horde. They came in waves of frenzied swarms, trying to get past Fathomir's defenders.

So far Striiker and the mariners from Riptide United were keeping them out. But they were losing sharkkind. Gray was worried. He never let on to the mariners or shiver sharks, but he couldn't see how they would get out of Fathomir, much less win.

"Can I speak with you?" Oceania asked.

Takiza shook his fins in irritation. "I am over five hundred years old. Do not treat me as you would a pup!"

Gray nodded to the surgeonfish. "He deserves to know."

She sighed. "I don't know what to do," Oceania began, looking over Takiza's injured flank. "The rips in his fins aren't the worst of it. Whatever vile force hit him, it's doing something. Something that I can't stop. The wound is getting worse."

"What does that mean?" Gray asked, his worry increasing.

"It means nothing!" Takiza said, stopping the surgeonfish from speaking. "Oceania, however well intentioned, doesn't know the ways of shar-kata.

I could not block all of Hokuu's power burst. Some small bit seeped past my shield. That is all."

Gray turned his bulk in the small cavern so he could get a better look at Takiza. He didn't look as bright as usual. His rainbow colors seemed to be melting into each other.

"He's correct about that," the surgeonfish said.

"So? So?" asked Gray. "What does that mean? You're not—you're not—" He couldn't bring himself to say the words.

"No, I am not!" Takiza huffed. The betta could see that Gray was unconvinced. "Rest assured I will be here to see many more of your training mistakes. I will slowly regain my health using shar-kata. Sometimes this requires going into a deep trance. But once we are in the open waters where I can feel the full healing powers of the tides, all will be well."

"You're sure," Gray prodded.

"I am," answered Takiza. "Go and complete your tasks. I will rest. The current is fine here. Would that make you both stop hovering over me like I'm a turtle hatchling?"

"It would be a start," Oceania said.

Gray nodded to Takiza and swam off, still troubled.

Thankfully there was a lull in the battle. He went into one of the deeper caverns, gliding on the current that filtered in from the front entrance.

In a moment Gray found his mother, Sandy, taking care of the shiver sharkkind and dwellers of Riptide. Nurse sharks were good at that. Lumos gave off light from their positions on the walls and down below the ancient reef. Mosses, lichens, and other cave greenies grew, giving the smaller dwellers a place to rest and feed.

"Hi, Mom," he said.

She must have seen something in his eyes because the barbels on the sides of her mouth vibrated. She called to Onyx, who was helping keep order. "Can you take over?" she asked the blacktip. "I'd like to speak with my son."

"Sure thing, Sandy," Onyx told her. He immediately shouted at a few older pups that were causing a stir. "Hey! What have I told you fin biters about snout-banging each other in the middle of everyone! Get over here!"

Gray and Sandy swam to a ledge below everyone else where they could be alone. They hovered where the current was stronger so they could breathe better. "Tell me how you're doing," she said, giving him a flank rub with her tail.

This felt wonderful and calmed him. Gray had thought he was too old to be so affected but apparently that wasn't true. "Well, our food supplies are low and Grimkahn keeps sending his frills to try to breach the main cavern—"

Sandy slashed her tail through the water. "I asked how *you* were doing, not how the battle is going."

Gray didn't have an answer. Finally he said, "Is there a difference?" Sandy shook her head as he continued. "I'm the Seazarein, Mom. I'm supposed to have all the answers. Everyone looks to me to lead. I don't think I'm allowed to say, 'Well, I feel a little down today. Maybe we could play tag-a-long until I feel better.'"

"You're a shark, Gray," Sandy chided. "You have feelings. You get to be sad. You get to laugh."

He forced a grin for his mom. "You're right. See? I'm all better."

"You know what I mean," Sandy said.

A dweller poked his head from the mossy greenie and for a moment Gray didn't know who it was. But then the colorful sea dragon opened its mouth.

"Hey, Gray!" Yappy said as his leafy fins moved with tiny micro-currents that only he could feel. "Sorry to listen in but I'm playing hide and seek with Riprap and Ebbie so I heard. They're really good by the way, but I miss the days when you and Barkley used to swim and play around the reef. Sandy's right, you need to smile more."

Gray chuckled. He couldn't believe Yappy was inside Fathomir. "How did you get here from Riptide's homewaters?"

"Oh, the quickfins help us slower dwellers with

directions if everyone leaves," Yappy said. "It took a while but I made it." Gray nodded in wonder. The journey for such a small dweller would have been staggering. "How's everything going with Grimkahn?" the little dragon asked.

"Well," Gray began. "We're safe now. That's all I can really say."

"You'll win," Yappy said, nodding solemnly. "You always do."

Gray looked at all the sharks jammed into the cavern. There were so many, and every single one was counting on him.

"Oh, and I delivered your message!" the sea dragon said.

Gray was confused. "What message?"

"To my cousins."

Gray still didn't know what the sea dragon was talking about. "You know, the message to my giant cousins from the deep waters of the Dark Blue. I couldn't go down there myself but I sent word. Once they hear about us—I mean, I did call them to help with Finnivus and he's gone—but these fins are worse so they're still needed. They'll come and help you beat all those dumb monsters keeping us in here. You, Takiza, Barkley, Striiker, and my cousins! You'll see!"

Yappy had spoken of his giant cousins that lived in the depths of the Dark Blue since they were pups. Supposedly, when Gray was fighting against

Finnivus's Black Wave armada, Yappy had sent a message for these imaginary giant sea dragons to come
help. But Yappy also had a theory that the moon above
the chop-chop was made of cheese.

Despite the situation Gray let out a barking laugh.
He couldn't help it.

"What's so funny?" said Yappy.

Gray couldn't think of anything to say and didn't
want to let the sea dragon know he had been laughing
at him. Thankfully Riprap and Ebbie saved him.

"Tag! Tag! Tag!" shouted Riprap, skimming by
Yappy and touching him with a fin.

"We found you!" added Ebbie.

"You did!" Yappy said. "You guys are definitely
the best finders ever!"

Riprap and Ebbie swam excitedly around Sandy
and Gray.

"We are awesome," said Riprap. "That's a fact."

Ebbie gave her brother a bump to the side. "Quit
being such a chowderhead! We only found him
because he was talking with Gray."

Yappy shook his head and fluttered his colorful
fins in disagreement. "No way! I was hiding *while*
talking! I was—"

Suddenly there was a tremendous rumble. It
seemed like the walls of the mountainous cavern were
collapsing.

"What's that?" asked Sandy fearfully.

"I don't know, Gray told her. "Stay here and make sure no one panics."

Gray swam out of the back cavern in a flash. The noise grew louder as he approached the throne area. Had Grimkahn figured out a way in? Was Hokuu using his power to blast a path inside?

"GET AWAY!" shouted Striiker. "CLEAR THE AREA!"

The rumbling grew, shaking the throne cavern violently. Gray saw boulders falling down outside. It didn't stop until Fathomir's entrance was totally blocked.

The noises stopped. The mariners and everyone else were silent.

Striiker quietly said, "I guess Grimkahn wasn't too keen on you sending that quickfin out."

"I guess so," Gray answered, staring at the wall of giant boulders.

They were sealed in.

In a moment the current slowed and then stopped. The cavern was large enough for them to survive for a little while.

But only a little. A half day at most.

If Gray didn't figure out how to escape, every one of them would suffocate.

CHAPTER 21

JUST OUTSIDE OF FATHOMIR TERRITORY Barkley watched as the guards circled in front of the greenie curtain that hid the Stingeroo Supper Club. The patterns they swam seemed random but definitely weren't. They were fiendishly complex and no area was ever unwatched for more than a minute. Yes, he and Velenka could easily swim the distance in less than that, but they couldn't do it without being seen.

"No way in without being caught," Velenka whispered, also noting the situation.

Barkley nodded but gave the mako a soft fin flick to the flank to be quiet.

She was smart. He would give her that.

Well, I didn't swim all this way for nothing, Barkley thought.

"What are you doing?" Velenka hissed as he left

the greenie and headed toward the Stingeroo entrance. He didn't get far before guards blocked his way.

"Club's closed," a bull shark told him. "Come back next week." The shark was older but swam with skill and no wasted motion. Probably an ex-mariner.

"I'm not here for the seasoned fish," Barkley said. "I'm here to see Trank."

Other guards spotted Velenka and surrounded her. "Got another one here, Rocko," yelled another guard, a big blue shark.

"Friend of yours?" asked Rocko, who was obviously in charge of this group.

Barkley nodded. "Yep. A setting for two would be nice."

Rocko smirked and led them inside. Stingeroo was deserted. They were swum to the center area of the club. Barkley saw that Ripper was with Trank.

"You didn't tell me he was going to be here!" Velenka said nervously when she spotted the battle-scarred hammerhead.

Velenka had betrayed a shiver leader named Goblin when Ripper had been his first. Barkley had forgotten that little fact but there was nothing he could do about it now. Velenka tried to hide herself among the guards but these ex-mariners—they had to be, they were very good—didn't allow it.

Ripper saw him first. "Doggie! What are you thinking coming—" The hammerhead stopped speaking when he saw Velenka. His eyes flashed with anger. "YOU!"

He was about to streak at her when Trank yelled, "Hold it! Everyone calm down!"

Ripper's fins and tail twitched in anger. "I'm so glad I get to see you again, Velenka. So, so glad."

"Take it easy, why don't youse," said Trank in his odd drawl. No one in the ocean spoke like the stonefish and not for the first time Barkley wondered where he was from.

Velenka hovered close to the old fins guarding her. She didn't want to give the hammerhead a shot at her gills. "Ripper, good to see you," she said, although plainly it was the last thing she was thinking. "I've always respected you, you know. You should have been the leader of the shiver. I always thought that."

"Why?" spat the big hammerhead. "So you could put a hit out on me? Yeah, I work for Trank. I hear things."

"Whoa, whoa," Trank said. "Let's not dredge up the past. What you doin' here, dogfish? I know you don't like my seasoned fish." Trank signaled the guards with a fin waggle and allowed Barkley to move forward.

"You know what I'm here for," he told the stonefish. "Gray's prepared to offer you a hunk of territory, including some of the golden greenie field for your help."

"Youse can't do anything with new territory if you're dead," the stonefish said.

Barkley flicked his fins but kept his temper under control. "Help us and you'll be paid well. We're in trouble."

"Not my problem."

Barkley slashed his tail through the water. "You're wrong. It's everyone's problem. You think you can ride this current out? No way. Grimkahn won't be satisfied with free seasoned fish."

Trank gave a noncommittal swish of his fins. "Maybe he's a music fan. We got great bands here. Youse never know."

"Oh come on!" Barkley said. "Do you really want to take that chance?"

"More than I want to take the chance of making him irate," Trank answered. "In case youse haven't noticed, I'm not sealed up inside of Fathomir like Gray and the rest of yer pals. I got my tailfin waving free here." The stonefish saw the confused look on Barkley's face. "Ain't been keepin' up on current events, have youse? I might not have quickfins, but I do pay good fish for information. Grimkahn's bruisers caused an avalanche. Fathomir's shut tighter than a clam. And youse wants me to risk my skin? Thanks, but no thanks."

"Even with that, it's still the right play," Velenka said.

"Definitely don't listen to this one," Ripper interrupted.

The mako swished her tail back and forth. "Sure. Don't listen. But I'm just like you, Trank. I look out for myself. And you should, too."

"Velenka!" shouted Barkley.

"Let me finish!" she insisted. "When the survivors of the horde tell everyone that you didn't flick a fin one way or the other during this war, everyone in the Big Blue will know it. You think business was bad when Finnivus took over? That'll make what's going to happen look like the good old days. No shark or dweller is coming to listen to music or eat with the traitorous fins that sided with the jurassics."

Barkley was amazed. Velenka had made an argument he would have never thought of and directed it at what Trank really cared about—his own personal power and wealth.

But the stonefish wasn't impressed. "Youse done?" he asked. "Sorry, dogfish. Made the swim out here for nuthin'."

"Yeah. What part of 'no' didn't you understand the first time?" Ripper added, staring at Velenka.

Barkley nodded. "You know I had to try."

The hammerhead turned to Trank. "Doggie and I have had our differences. Heck, I even thought about sending him to the Sparkle Blue once or twice. I've let go of that. But Velenka is something else. You better believe she could cause trouble later. Let me have her."

Trank studied Velenka. "She turned on me once, too. I ever tell you that?"

"I don't doubt it," said Ripper.

The mako's huge black eyes seemed to grow even bigger. "That—that was an unfortunate decision on my part. I—I wasn't—it wasn't my fault."

"Trank," Barkley said evenly. "We came here to talk. We came in peace."

The stonefish stared at Velenka, considering. "Yeah Barkley, but you're lookin' out for your friends. I get that. I *respect* that. Velenka here, she don't look out for no one but herself. Maybe it's time for her to swim off to the Sparkle Blue."

"Exactly what I was thinking," Ripper said with a gleam in his eye.

"Salamanca thinks that would be a grave mistake," said a huge blue marlin. Everyone looked to the side where he, Jaunt, twenty AuzyAuzy mariners, Snork, and a huge narwhal with a giant, sharp horn hovered. The group had somehow slipped past the guards.

Ripper shouted, "Paddletail, Dorno! Sound off!"

The narwhal, easily the largest fin—or more correctly, flipper—glided forward. He wasn't menacing them with his pointy tusk, but then he didn't have to. "Your guards are alive and only their pride is hurt."

"Easy boys," Trank said to the guards. "Don't want any trouble in my place just when I got it lookin' the way I like." He motioned at the newcomers. "I'm Trank, the manager of this humble establishment. Might I interest youse in a serving of the finest seasoned fish the Sific has to offer?"

"Really?" asked Salamanca. "Salamanca loves seasoned fish. How is it prepared here?"

"Not now, you wonky drongo!" said Jaunt. "Barkley, you okay?"

"We're all right," he said.

Velenka interrupted. "No, we're not! They want to *kill* me!"

"Whoa, whoa!" said Trank. "I was only thinkin' out loud and hadn't made a decision. Now I have. If Gray didn't send youse to the Sparkle Blue, who am I to do it?"

"NO!" shouted Ripper. "We can take 'em!"

Trank snapped his little tail, and it was louder than Barkley would have thought possible. "Ripper, you're a good fin, but my decision is final. Let it go or it's time for you to swim away from here."

The hammerhead studied the gathered force allied against him. Even the guards he was in charge of moved away. Ripper gave Trank a stiff nod. "Fine."

"Was what you said about Gray being trapped true?" asked the narwhal.

"It sure is," the stonefish said. "Those mosasaurs sent boulders bouncing down the side of the mountain and sealed everyone inside. Gotta be gettin' stuffy in there. If you're gonna do something, sooner is better."

"We got problems," Jaunt said.

"More problems," Aleeyoot added.

Trank swished his tail at the big marlin. "Salamanca, is it? You talk kinda funny."

"Oh, *he* talks funny," Barkley said, rolling his eyes.

The blue marlin pointed his bill at Trank and his eyes narrowed on the small dweller. "Is that so? Does the way Salamanca speaks amuse you, stonefish? Does it make you laugh?"

Everyone went silent. Jaunt backed away. "Now you've gone and done it," she said.

"No, not like that," Trank said. "I mean no disrespect. But the only Salamanca I ever heard of that speaks in the third person is a bladefish that swims the waters of the northern Atlantis on the Europa side."

Salamanca dipped his bill with a circular flourish. "Yes, that is me."

Trank turned to Jaunt and the narwhal. "And you're a narwhal. Only bladefish narwhal I ever heard of is called Aleeyoot. That youse?"

"Why do you want to know?" asked Aleeyoot.

Trank waved his fins in a soothing manner. "AuzyAuzy and their fins are tight with Gray, so I get why they're here. But youse bladefish? I thought youse didn't mess with power struggles in the Big Blue, kinda like me. After all, youse didn't come in against Finnivus."

Salamanca and Jaunt watched Aleeyoot as he thought this over. After a moment he said, "You're right. We don't usually get involved in wars between shivers. In the end, Finnivus was from the Big Blue. Cruel and evil, yes. But life would have gone on. This threat is different. We felt we had to choose a side."

"Some of us decided before others that it was the right thing to do," Salamanca said with a grin.

Trank nodded. "Very enlightening. Best of luck to youse, then."

Barkley turned to the relieved Velenka and everyone began to swim away.

From behind them they heard Trank add, "And Salamanca, if youse guys end up winning, the seasoned fish is on the house."

CHAPTER 22

GRAY HOVERED IN A SMALLER CAVERN WHERE he had ordered a meeting of his council. One way or another it would be their last meeting. The situation was dismal. With only a trickle of current flowing into Fathomir, they had precious little time left before everyone suffocated.

Takiza seemed better and for that Gray was thankful. Sandy and Onyx were also there, ready to receive instructions for the shiver sharks. Striiker and his subcommanders kept to themselves. Though the constant attacks had stopped because they were sealed in, the great white's planning for what they would do if freed did not. Tydal and Xander were also close, along with Leilani. She wasn't a mariner but Gray valued her opinion, as he did the others. It was also a comfort to have her by his side. He had sent Judijoan to distribute what little food they had left to the hungriest pups and older fins.

Gray didn't need anyone to run this meeting. He would do it himself.

"Okay, everyone," he said in a strong voice. "Listen up." All eyes in the cavern went to him. A year ago this would have been uncomfortable for Gray, but after so many dire situations, those feelings had passed. He was the Seazarein and he would lead. "Grimkahn has given us two choices. Stay in here and swim the Sparkle Blue or wriggle our way out of the cavern entrance to be eaten one by one. I don't like either of those."

"Right on, Gray!" shouted Striiker. "Tell us how we get to bloody their snouts."

Gray didn't look at Takiza but he could feel the betta's eyes on him. "I'm going to tunnel us out the other side of the mountain using shar-kata."

Everyone was quiet. It wasn't the rousing reception he was hoping for.

Finally, Xander put it into words. "Gray, I've seen Hokuu and Takiza scrumble with shar-kata, firing those bursts and bolts. Powerful, yeah, too right it is. But strong enough to cut through this mountain? Not a chance, mate. If the back is anything like the front entrance, it'll be fifty or even seventy feet of solid rock. That's impossible."

"That would be the case normally. But there is a way to amplify my strength many, many times," Gray said.

"No!" shouted Takiza. "Surely you do not mean to—"

Gray whirled. "The Seazarein Emprex is speaking and—with all respect—you *will* listen." His master quieted as Gray continued. "I can mix my life force with shar-kata to increase its power. It will not only dig through the side of Fathomir, but make a hole large enough so that we can swim whole battle fins out."

"Brilliant!" exclaimed Xander. "If we can keep the mariners in battle fins of a hundred we can assemble our formation right quick."

Striiker nodded. "It could work. We'd be on the other side from where Grimkahn's uglies are swimming. It would take them time to stack and face us."

"Foolishness!" said the betta.

"Takiza, my mind is made up."

Tydal gave Gray a fin flick, studying him. "I take it by Takiza's reaction that what you're attempting is dangerous."

The betta could remain quiet no longer. "Not only is it dangerous, it is idiotic!" Takiza looked at Gray and softened. "It is also very brave."

Gray was totally calm. He was more at ease with this decision than many others he had had to make. "Yes. It's dangerous. But only to me."

"Wait, what?" asked Striiker. "What do you mean? What'll happen to you?"

"I'm going to free you, is what's going to happen," Gray answered, not meeting anyone's eyes.

There was a long silence. Finally Leilani asked, "Do you mean that to free us you might . . . die?"

Gray gave his friends a tight smile.

He heard his mother whisper "Oh, no," and then everyone was yelling at once. Voices rang off the walls until Gray thought the cavern would collapse.

He amplified his voice with a shar-kata boost. The cavern was small and the result was deafening. "SILENCE!" He went on in his normal voice. "This is the only current we have left to swim. Any other time Takiza would do it." Gray looked warmly at his teacher. "But he can't. And I don't want him to. He's given enough through the years. This is my job. And who knows, maybe I won't need every bit of my life force to free us and we'll be laughing about this later. But the fact remains, we have to get out of here and then win the fight against Grimkahn and his jurassic horde. We are out of options and I, as Seazarein Emprex, am going to do this."

"There must be some other way," Leilani said, her eyes leaking tears into the water. Gray could taste them as they wafted through the space.

Striiker hid his distress, but only barely. "What are your orders, Seazarein?"

"I want you and Xander to get the mariners lined up, ten by ten," Gray began. "Some of them won't have seen this much power being used so you'll need to tell them what to expect. It's going to be bright and loud. Also, if the jurassics are patrolling, and they likely are, they will hear it. You should plan on only having a few minutes before Grimkahn comes at you with his entire force."

Gray turned to the others in the cavern. "Mom and Onyx, I want you to divide the shiver sharkkind and dwellers into smaller groups. These will swim away after the opening is made and the mariners have left. They'll have a better chance if they leave during the confusion of the fighting. Tydal, I need you to organize everything else inside the cavern. Gather the older and less injured mariners to protect any who can't leave, because Grimkahn might send frills in after our mariners are outside."

"Of course," the brown and yellow epaulette shark said, and dipped his snout.

"You have your orders," Gray said. "I begin in fifteen minutes at the cavern farthest in back. Please, move with a purpose."

This got everyone zipping in all directions, except Leilani, who remained by his side.

"I'm staying with you," the spinner said.

"No, you're not," Gray answered, shaking his head. "I need you to get the word out in case the worst happens. I need you to find BenzoBenzo or whoever's in charge of the spyfish Eyes and Ears. If we fail I want them to have all the information about Grimkahn, Hokuu, and the horde that might be useful. Then maybe someone else can defeat them."

"Oh, Gray," Leilani sobbed. But she couldn't say anything else and swam off.

Gray hovered alone in the cavern, listening to the roar of action he had set in motion.

He felt strangely at peace. The worrying, training, and waiting were finally over.

One way or another, everything would be decided.

"Have I ever told you that you are my most troublesome apprentice?" asked Takiza. The little betta drifted down in front of his left eye.

"Once or twice, Shiro," Gray sighed. "Once or twice."

"Come, I will help you focus your mind for this task," the betta told him. "You will need to be your best."

Gray nodded and they began.

It wouldn't be long now.

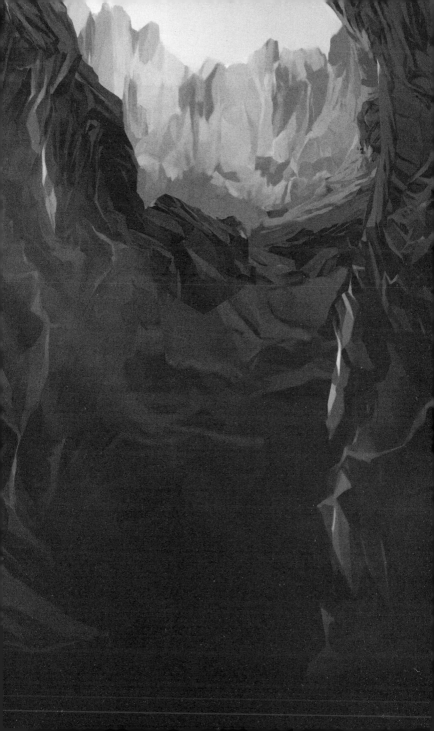

BREAKOUT

CHAPTER 23

THE RIPTIDE UNITED MARINERS WERE LINED up in squares of ten by ten, one battle fin of a hundred after another, nineteen in all. Nineteen hundred shark-kind was a large force, but there had been even more before the battle at Pax Shiver. Nearly three thousand.

Gray hoped that Barkley could convince Trank to help, but what were the tiny poisonous dwellers going to do against huge frilled sharks and even larger mosasaurs? Maybe Jaunt was waiting to join them with AuzyAuzy forces. But how many of them had survived Grimkahn's attack? And had Eugene Speedmeister delivered his message? Was he even alive?

We'll have to do this alone, Gray thought.

"ATTEN-SHUN HOVER!" shouted Striiker. The rows of Riptide United mariners went fins up. "SPLIT RANKS!" The mariners made a space between the fifth and sixth rows, creating a path so Gray could swim to the cavern wall.

Sharkkind tails and dorsals were urchin spine straight.

Not a fin was out of place.

Gray's heart swelled with pride.

The lumos had been told what was going on. Other small dwellers like shellbacks and turtles had carried them from the area Gray would attempt to bore through. He didn't want to lose any innocent lives when it could be avoided. Those that remained on the cavern ceiling, walls, and pillars of volcanic rock shone brighter than Gray had ever seen. The colors were breathtaking as he began the slow swim past his fighting sharkkind to attempt the impossible.

Tyro, give me strength, he thought.

Gray met the eyes of the mariners that would swim out to battle Grimkahn and his horde should he succeed. They were ready to die to save the Big Blue.

Gray would *not* let them down.

If he had to use all his life force, so be it.

"CLOSE RANKS!" bellowed Striiker when Gray passed through the formation. "FINS UP AND AT THE READY!"

Gray reached out with his senses, falling deeper into concentration than he ever had before. He saw and felt everything: the heartbeats of the mariners, the electricity that formed the lumo lights, all things down to the tiniest wisps of moss pushed back and forth by the micro-currents that still flowed through Fathomir.

He asked the water and the rocks forming Fathomir to allow him to use their power, just for a little while. The reception he received was a warm one, and Gray felt more connected to the Big Blue than at any time in his entire life. The energy of the waters flowed into him, making everything so very bright to his eyes. He added his own life force to this and the power inside him multiplied and blossomed.

Gray kept the force churning and growing until he could bear no more. It crackled and popped in the water all around him. He was glowing now, heat coming from inside him. It only happened when the amount of power you were channeling was massive.

With a shout he released what he had gathered.

A stream of energy poured from Gray and turned the rock it touched into sand. He moved forward, making sure the dust didn't spread in the water and choke his mariners. He put every ounce of his will into it. Gray's heightened senses told him exactly how much rock he would have to cut through to get outside.

It wasn't fifty or even seventy feet.

It was a hundred and two.

Too far, too far . . .

I will not fail! he shouted inside his mind.

The first fifty feet of rock disappeared in a flash of light.

Then twenty more.

Gray mixed the energy of the ocean with his life force and kept shooting it forward.

It felt like he was on fire with twenty-five feet to go.

Then it was twenty.

Fifteen.

Gray's progress slowed.

It took more time to move the next five feet than it had to cut through everything else.

Ten feet of rock remained between them and the revitalizing waters of the Big Blue.

Gray gritted his teeth, driving more and more of his life force into his effort.

Eight feet . . .

His sight began to dim.

Six feet . . .

Sparkles blipped into existence everywhere. These weren't like the white lights that you found with shar-kata. They were colorful.

Three feet . . .

He had to finish! He would not allow everyone to die without a fighting chance!

Gray took the last of his life force, transferring it into his effort to vaporize the last of the rock in front of him. He had to get through or they would die.

But it wasn't enough.

There was still a foot of solid rock in front of him and he could not break it down!

Darkness closed in. The lights around Gray grew brighter and more colorful.

It was the Sparkle Blue.

He saw the dim shapes of sharkkind swimming between colorful flashes.

Were some of the sharks calling to him?

They were!

Gray wanted to swim over to them, but then . . . he got stronger. The dimness and colorful lights receded. He began to feel refreshed. Gray's body, his soul, latched onto the power and soaked it in. He realized it could only be coming from one place.

Or more accurately, one fin.

Takiza.

The foolish betta was draining *his* life force and pouring it into Gray to keep him alive.

Sure enough he found the betta floating above his snout. "I never said I wouldn't help. Now, what are you waiting for?"

Nothing!

Gray blasted through the final foot of rock, vaporizing it. He shot forward into the open water, breathing deep of the cold current, which tasted so sweet it made him want to laugh and cry all at once. He moved to the side as Striiker and Xander led their mariners through the gap.

"MOVE, MOVE, MOVE!" shouted the great white.

Gray turned to speak to Takiza, but the betta was gone in the mad rush of nineteen battle fins of mariners pouring from the Fathomir mountainside.

Jaunt couldn't believe it when the mountainside disappeared in a flash of brightness and Gray swam out.

He was literally shining with power!

Jaunt had hidden her battle fins in the golden greenie field on one side of Fathomir. After they returned from Trank's and saw with their own eyes how Gray and his forces were trapped, their hopes had dimmed. How could they possibly get them out? She, Barkley, Salamanca, and Aleeyoot were in the middle of a heated argument when Gray had made his own way.

She rushed up and nudged him on the flank. She had to dodge because, thinking he was being attacked, Gray almost tail slapped her into the next week. But he regained his senses quickly and was getting stronger every minute.

"Glad to see you, ya big beauty!" she told him.

"Me too, Jaunt," Gray replied. "But let's save the group rubs until later."

Jaunt gave Gray a fin flick. "What do you need me to do?"

"Join your mariners to our formation," Gray said.

"We can't sort everyone in time! We'll do more harm than good."

Gray shook his head and pointed at Striiker, busily giving orders. "No sorting. We're using each armada like a battle fin, so really you'll be a separate unit. You can break off before first contact with you leading your group."

Jaunt nodded. "That's different, all right. On my way!" She yelled to her subcommanders, "Shake those tails, Golden Rush! We got us a scrumble to win!"

There was a cheer from her mariners. They were itching for the chance to fight Grimkahn on more even terms. Striiker put her mariners on top of the formation. Jaunt was getting everything ready as best she could when she caught sight of the jurassic horde.

It was all of them, and they blackened the waters as they came around the mountainside.

Hokuu watched the scene unfold before his eyes. He had felt the shar-kata being used and moved to get a better view when the breach in the mountainside appeared. The amount of energy necessary to do this was immense. Gray would be drained.

Now was the time to strike!

But Hokuu didn't see Takiza, and his old Nulo had to be somewhere close.

No, Hokuu wouldn't rush in.

And he didn't have to.

The mountain had rumbled as Gray burned his way through it. Frilled shark scouts were alerted and reported to Grimkahn. The mosasaur king and his mighty horde weren't caught completely by surprise. Even now they were swimming at the Riptide mariners who still needed time to get into formation.

The battle waters would run red with blood!

Hokuu would let Grimkahn and Gray fight it out.

That way there would be only one enemy left.

One weakened enemy that would be ripe for the taking.

All he had to do was wait.

And I'll get to watch one heck of a fight, he thought.

What could be better? Hokuu settled in to enjoy the carnage.

CHAPTER 24

GRAY TOOK A POSITION UNDERNEATH Striiker. It would be foolish to lead the attack himself. He wasn't in this for personal glory. He wanted to win. And their best chance was with Striiker directing the battle from the diamondhead. But that didn't mean he would let the great white and the other mariners fight without him.

Grimkahn's roar tore through the water with an almost physical force. The jurassic horde lumbered forward, set in their massive block formation.

It was a fearsome sight.

"Steady on in the ranks!" Striiker shouted. "Increase speed to twenty-five!"

Olph the battle dolph clicked out the order. Jaunt's AuzyAuzy mariners were massed on top of their force's rectangle shape. Riptide United occupied the center and Xander commanded the bottom AuzyAuzy and Indi Shiver sharkkind.

Gray was missing the adrenaline surge that coursed through him before a battle. It must have been due to all the energy he expended freeing them from Fathomir.

Thankfully he felt fine otherwise.

Good thing I'm still pretty big, he thought.

"KILL THEM ALL!" shouted Grimkahn. "NO MERCY!"

"RAMMING SPEED!" answered Striiker.

The two gigantic formations sped toward each other.

Less than twenty tail strokes away, Striiker cried, "Split!"

Instantly, the three armadas followed the individual instructions of Jaunt, Striiker, and Xander. The battle dolphins above each commander used a burst of click-razz at the sharkkind in those armadas.

Jaunt took her mariners, swung to the side, and dove downward.

Striiker led Gray and Riptide to the right.

And Xander's forces shot straight up and out of the immediate fight.

But Grimkahn was also prepared.

His own horde split into two halves. One went snout-to-snout with Jaunt's forces and the other went after Riptide. In less than a second Gray found himself in the fight of his life. He couldn't see anything as red, red blood clouded the water. Their force had planned to only strike glancing blows against the horde after splitting their mega-armada but Grimkahn's maneuver had complicated that.

And they were taking so many casualties!

But while Grimkahn had done some training, the horde wasn't nearly as good at formation fighting as they were.

And we have three armadas, Gray thought.

A moment later Xander's force blasted into Grimkahn's monsters from above, executing a Reverse Spinner Strikes. Xander had brilliantly split his own armada into two halves to hit each section of the divided jurassic horde from the top. The mariners were told they would not be able to take out the mosasaurs while the frills protected them, so every sharkkind went after the frilled shark in its path.

The fighting was chaos and fury with sharkkind, frills, and giant mosasaurs striking every which way in close combat. So many mariners spiraled from the battle on their way to the Sparkle Blue it felt like Gray was breathing blood instead of water.

If it weren't for Xander's attack from above, they would have lost in the first minute. But still, Riptide and Jaunt's forces were stuck fast in close combat and couldn't free themselves even with Xander's disruptive attack.

They were being eaten alive and couldn't break away!

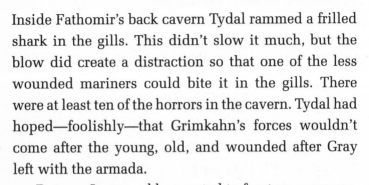

Inside Fathomir's back cavern Tydal rammed a frilled shark in the gills. This didn't slow it much, but the blow did create a distraction so that one of the less wounded mariners could bite it in the gills. There were at least ten of the horrors in the cavern. Tydal had hoped—foolishly—that Grimkahn's forces wouldn't come after the young, old, and wounded after Gray left with the armada.

But, no. It seemed he wanted to feast on everyone.

Sandy and Onyx had been able to evacuate half of the shiver sharks before the attackers struck. An entire group of fifty shiver sharkkind was sent to the Sparkle Blue when frills descended on them. Whole families were mauled, young and old.

Tydal had created a small unit of the least wounded mariners before their fighting sharks had left for the main battle. But all had injuries severe enough to keep them from fighting with the armada. Gray couldn't spare a single healthy shark to remain inside Fathomir.

"Fight!" he yelled to the mariners at his flanks. "Fight for your lives!"

The frilled sharks whipsawed through the water like greenie in a rough current. Their attacks were deadly, especially their barbed tails, which struck home time and time again.

Tydal tried to bite one the beasts in the flank and was tail slapped so hard he was thrown out of the battle. He was an epaulette shark and not very fierce, but everyone was needed. The only reason they weren't dead already was because the hole Gray created was plugged by mariners who knew how to stay in formation and fight.

But those weakened and wounded sharks were being sent to the Sparkle Blue at a terrifying rate. The enemy moved forward, biting and slashing their way through the Fathomir defenders. The attackers were picking up speed and pushing everyone backward. If the frills got out of the tunnel and into the larger cavern where they could use their agility to its fullest, Tydal and everyone else were finished.

"Stop them!" shouted Tydal. "Don't let them inside!"

Then in one disastrous swoop ten of their wounded mariners got sent to the Sparkle Blue.

The defensive line crumbled.

The monsters were going to get inside and kill everyone.

Suddenly someone shouted "Chaaarge!" and there was the sound of a hundred fins racing madly above Tydal.

He turned as Gray's little brother and sister— Riprap and Ebbie were their names, he remembered— streaked over his head leading a mass of *pups* straight at the frills.

"No!" Tydal cried, but it was too late.

The young sharks drove into the thick of the battle. It surprised the frilled sharks long enough that the wounded mariners were able to score many mortal hits.

The tide had turned!

With one last rush the pups and mariners drove the frills from the cavern.

"I told you we could do it!" cried Riprap.

"No!" countered Ebbie. "*I* told you!"

The older mariners reorganized and put themselves in a strong defensive line.

They were safe for now.

But what of the battle outside?

"We are out of time!" shouted Salamanca. "They are dying out there!" The big marlin pointed with his bill at the seething melee. Snork watched the battle waters with horror. Until this point Aleeyoot had wanted them to wait. But time was running out for his friends and everyone else.

"I guess we have no choice," said the narwhal. "I was hoping for a distraction so we could single out the mosasaurs without having to fight our way through the frilled sharks."

"No matter! All these monsters need killing!" said Salamanca.

Aleeyoot nodded his long and straight tusk. "You're right."

The narwhal turned to give the order but Snork saw something in the distance. "Wait! Over there!" Unseen by those in the fight, a triangular mass swam toward the battle. "Sharkkind!" he said.

But then Snork noticed that some of them were too big to be sharks.

"Monsters are swimming with them!" said Salamanca as he and Aleeyoot peered into the distance.

Snork froze. If it was more frilled sharks, they would lose for sure.

But they weren't allies of Grimkahn and the jurassics. They were orcas!

"That's Tik-Tun and the orcas of Icingholme Shiver," Snork said, excited. "They've come to help!"

Aleeyoot tapped Salamanca. "Perfect. They'll strike from behind and create that distraction."

Salamanca poked Aleeyoot in a friendly way and grinned. "And we come from below, no? Slaying the mosasaurs as you proposed, my most excellent narwhal friend."

"I'm the only narwhal you know, Salamanca."

"It still counts," the marlin answered. "We go!"

A shouted order later and Snork was streaming with the other bladefish into the battle waters. They stayed low in the tall greenie, keeping hidden as long as they could. Through the waving golden kelp, Snork saw the sharkkind and orcas rip into the jurassic formation. This added at least another thousand sharks and two hundred orcas to the raging battle. The fighting was so frenzied Snork didn't see how any of them would live through it.

The mosasaurs were too big to be taken down by mariner bite. A shark's jaws just weren't large enough to do mortal damage. But bladefish had pointy weapons that could reach something vital if they were clever.

And Snork was proud that every bladefish he had met was *very* clever.

"Stay close, oh mighty Snork!" said Salamanca. "Today you become a legend!" The giant marlin wasn't afraid at all. He was eager.

Snork wished he was half as brave, because he was scared out of his mind.

"Keep low!" shouted Aleeyoot. "Wait until we're right under them!" Though shouting wasn't a smart thing to do if you wanted to remain hidden, the sounds of the battle above were deafening and masked the noise they made.

Snork did his best to keep up but it seemed that everyone was faster. By far, most of the bladefish were marlins, spearfish, sailfish, and swordfish—all known for their speed. The halfbeaks and needlefish were smaller but also whipped through the water with ease. Even Aleeyoot managed to be at the front of the pack and he was a *narwhal*. Snork was the only saw-fish. He kept his eyes straight ahead and swam with all his might.

Then the order came. "Now!" said Aleeyoot, and their entire group ripped a turn straight up that caused the fish Snork had eaten a day ago to slap from one side to the other inside his belly.

After four tail strokes, Snork entered the battle.

It was horrible.

Blood was everywhere and caused him to gag.

Sharks were torn apart, some even swallowed whole by the mosasaurs.

Salamanca weaved through them like a madfin, shouting things like, "Have at you, monster! Today is your last!" and "You are as ugly as you are unskilled!"

The big blue marlin didn't slow as he chopped his way through three frilled sharks and found a mosasaur flipper. He sliced it clean off. Then he did a fancy pirouette and chopped another one, sending the prehistore monster careening away in agony. Snork was caught underneath the mosasaur's bulk for a moment. He managed to swim free before it crashed into the seabed, crushing an unlucky frill underneath it.

Another frilled shark reared in front of Snork. He blocked a tail strike and then slashed at its neck. It wasn't a good cut, but blood spurted everywhere and

Snork moved past as the creature thrashed in its death agony.

With his long tusk, Aleeyoot was as deadly as Salamanca. He didn't yell like the blue marlin, but the frilled sharks must have sensed he was dangerous and tried to avoid him. Any of them in range of his nine-foot horn was sent to the Sparkle Blue. He then evaded the snap of a mosasaur before diving underneath the giant. When the mosasaur opened its crocodile mouth to try again, Aleeyoot cut its lower jaw off.

Two frills attacked Aleeyoot from behind, and Salamanca—lightning fast—cut them both in half. "That makes four times Salamanca has saved your life!" he said, waggling his bill triumphantly.

"It was *one* attack!" disagreed Aleeyoot as he skewered another frill with his tusk.

"There were two enemies to be slain!"

Aleeyoot sent another frilled shark to the Sparkle Blue. "No way!"

"Let us agree to disagree!" shouted Salamanca. "But I am right! Four!"

Snork fought another frilled shark, this one coming forward with a series of tail attacks. Though the noise of battle all around him was riotous, he heard the high-pitched whine of the spike passing by his ear as if it were the only sound in the ocean. If he survived this battle, he doubted he would ever forget it. Three more times the frilled shark shot his tail at him and three times Snork blocked until he landed a counter, sending the frill sinking to the seabed.

"GIVE THEM NOTHING!" he heard Striiker yell in his booming voice from twenty feet away.

Striiker was there! His friend was alive!

But a mosasaur had gotten above him and the great white didn't see the danger. Even the dolphin that usually protected Striiker's dorsal was occupied, ramming another frill that Striiker was fighting with his blunt snout.

Snork accelerated as fast as he could.

It came down to a matter of an inch.

Striiker would have been bitten in half, but Snork pierced the huge mosasaur's eye with his blade as he reared back to bite. With a twist Snork pulled his blade free and the monster sank without a sound. The great white stared in shock as the mosasaur slipped from view. "Glad you could join the party, pal!" he told Snork.

He and Striiker fought, flank to flank.

Snork still didn't see how any of them would survive the day.

CHAPTER 25

BARKLEY HAD HOPED TO JOIN JAUNT'S AUZYAUZY mariners for the battle but was turned away because Velenka was with him. AuzyAuzy didn't like the mako since she had swum with Finnivus when his armada destroyed their homewaters. Salamanca and Aleeyoot hadn't let Barkley set out with the bladefins because they thought it was suicide for him. Barkley had to admit that to thrust himself in the middle of a melee without a sharp snout as a close-quarter weapon probably wasn't his best idea ever. So he and Velenka were lurking on the edges of the battle waters deep in the greenie looking for Hokuu.

So far they had seen no sign of the evil frilled shark.

Barkley felt absolutely useless as sharkkind died by the scores above him.

He couldn't help any of them!

Though the fury of the battle drowned everything out Velenka kept her voice low. "Hokuu's here. Close."

"How do you know?" asked Barkley.

"Because he wouldn't miss this," she said. "I still don't believe he and Grimkahn had an actual fight, but either way, he's here."

Even if the fight had been real, Hokuu could be waiting for the perfect time to betray the mosasaur king if he won. The frill's wound was authentic enough. Barkley watched Grimkahn roar and chop a mariner in half with his huge crocodile mouth. He seemed unstoppable.

Suddenly Grimkahn darted off to the side and out of the immediate fight.

Why?

Barkley moved to get a better view.

"What are you doing?" Velenka hissed. "Keep down!"

Grimkahn snapped at something but the mosasaur's body blocked Barkley's view of what it was.

Then Barkley saw it was Gray.

"What is that chowderheaded fool doing?" asked Velenka when she saw.

Gray got slapped by Grimkahn's huge tail. He was dazed.

"Stay here!" Barkley said and he jetted forward as fast as he could. He wouldn't let Gray be eaten without doing *something*. "HEY! HEY! HEY!" was all Barkley could think to shout. Grimkahn heard and glanced his way.

The mosasaur didn't stop, though. He rushed at the stunned Gray, opening his lethal jaws.

Barkley did the only thing he could think of. . . .

He tail-finned Grimkahn in the eye.

Barkley apparently hit his mark because the mosasaur lunged at him with a pained screech. The jurassic was amazingly quick for something so big.

Gray slipped away into the thick of battle. He hadn't even seen Barkley's charge.

But Grimkahn had.

Now Barkley was about to get eaten, when—

Velenka *swam through* Grimkahn's mouth and out the other side!

This distracted the mosasaur king so much that he fouled his flipper strokes and reflexively struck at Velenka. The small delay allowed Barkley time to madly swim forward. When Grimkahn bit down—missing by an urchin spine—a wave of water forced Barkley forward as the mosasaur's huge jaws slammed behind him.

The *only* reason he was alive was because of Velenka's distraction. . . .

Barkley tumbled into the greenie as Grimkahn resumed his pursuit of Gray.

"Well that was the dumbest thing I've ever done," Velenka said. She twisted and saw the tip of her tail-fin was missing. It was only an inch, but still. She chuckled nervously. "They don't get much closer than that, do they?"

"I guess I owe you a few trust points," Barkey said.

"Only a few?" she asked, faking displeasure. "I just swam through Grimkahn's mouth for you!"

"I know you did," Barkley said.

"Youse was both pretty brave there," said the familiar voice of Trank. "Stupid. But pretty brave. Maybe Gray and I were right about not sending you to the Sparkle Blue."

Ripper was also there, guarding Trank. The big hammerhead looked at Velenka and grunted, "Not bad. Let's not get carried away, either."

Barkley couldn't believe his eyes. "What are you two doing here?"

"Just taking a little swim," the stonefish said. "Gotta keep up the exercise when youse get to be my age."

Barkley then saw a mass of glowing . . . *something*. They weren't sharks. It was like a huge clump of lumo greenie caught in the current and heading straight for the fight.

Was Takiza up to something?

No. They were jellyfish!

They were different types and some of them were huge. Barkley remembered the names of a few: purple striped, moon, mauve stinger, sea nettle, and the giant lion's mane jelly, trailing tentacles longer than even a mosasaur.

The jellies drifted through the battle and by the reaction of those in the jurassic horde, scared the heck out of them. Striiker and their allies were able to get some space from the frilled sharks and mosasaurs and reform their mega-armada.

Then, as quickly as they came, the jellyfish were gone.

Barkley turned to Trank. "You did that, didn't you? I knew you cared."

"Whoa! Whoa!" said Trank, circling his fins in an annoyed way. "Don't go saying anything youse can't take back. I was taking a swim and happened to be here when that odd thing happened. I'm on no one's side. I do like your friends the bladefish though. They have style. And one of them saved my grandfather. Old family story, maybe I'll tell ya sometime. Well, I gotta get back to the club. Got some fish waiting to be seasoned. See ya 'round."

Ripper gave Barkley a wink and left with Trank.

Was this a dream?

Was he swimming the Sparkle Blue inside Grimkahn's stomach?

Barkley couldn't sort it out right now. His side hurt like it was covered with lava, and everyone above them began fighting again. He motioned to Velenka and they swam into the greenie to search for Hokuu once more.

Barkley even let Velenka cover his tail.

Gray was lucky he hadn't been eaten. He had been pushed past the main battle when Grimkahn saw him and attacked. Stupidly, Gray didn't think the mosasaur king was quick enough to hit him with a tail strike and he was knocked senseless for a moment.

Barkley had saved his life and then disappeared.

That's something else he'll never let me forget, thought Gray as he dodged another rush by Grimkahn. Gray had to make sure he didn't go back into the main battle and reappeared so the mosasaur king could see and chase him instead. He had recovered enough to use shar-kata but did not have anywhere near enough power to dent Grimkahn's armored hide. Right now Gray was swimming for his life.

"It's only a matter of time, pup!" the mosasaur king yelled as they paused from their exertions, both panting.

"Call your horde off, Grimkahn," Gray answered, keeping his distance. He could see that mariners were dying by the hundreds again after the giant jellyfish swarm had stopped the killing for a moment. The jurassic horde was inflicting huge losses once more. "You and I can fight for leadership! Or are you scared?"

Grimkahn laughed and it sounded like a rock slide. "You'd like that, wouldn't you? But I ordered my commanders not to stop fighting for *any* reason. You'll all be lunch today!" With that the mosasaur roared toward him again.

Gray gathered power with shar-kata and mixed it with a little of his life force. He felt his heart flutter and skip a beat as fire surged inside him.

FHWOOM!

The blast slowed the mosasaur king.

He stared at Gray and then began to laugh. "Pretty good, but still not enough! Hokuu thought he was going to send me to the Sparkle Blue like that, too. I wish he was around so I could kill you both at once. I told you. Nothing cuts through mosasaur hide but mosasaur teeth, and you're no mosasaur!"

Gray's heart sank. There wasn't anything he could do to injure Grimkahn.

He barely dodged the mosasaur's next strike.

But he wasn't fast enough to avoid the devastating snout ram that followed.

Gray listed to the left, sure his ribs were broken.

Grimkahn opened his mouth wide and snapped down on Gray.

"NOOO!" cried Leilani when she saw Grimkahn devour Gray.

It couldn't be!

Gray—the Seazarein—her friend . . . was gone.

Striiker fought furiously, barely keeping at bay the frilled shark who was trying to skewer his head with its tail.

Over the monster's shoulder he saw Gray and Grimkahn fighting.

Then Gray was gone.

There's no way, Striiker thought. Gray must have moved away with shar-kata speed and I missed it.

But where was he?

And why was Grimkahn howling with joy?

Barkley blinked, hoping that his eyes were lying.

His friend had been swallowed whole by Grimkahn.

My friend is dead, he thought.

Grimkahn roared in triumph, shaking the battle waters around him.

"I'VE WON!" he cried as he gnashed his teeth back and forth.

The chunky pup was made of tough stuff, Grimkahn would give him that.

Even now Gray's carcass was stuck tight in his throat.

But something was wrong.

There was no blood.

Blood always gushed pleasingly in his throat when he crushed the life out of prey.

Where was the blood?

Gray thought he was incredibly calm given the fact that he was entirely inside Grimkahn's mouth.

His shield glowed with power, but it was cracking. He could feel it beginning to give way to the incredible force of the mosasaur king's grinding teeth.

He couldn't dodge Grimkahn's last attack. He had known that.

It was then, a split second before the giant, toothy mouth closed on him, that Gray got an idea.

It was his craziest—and maybe best—yet.

He couldn't beat Grimkahn with his own size and speed. The monster was too big.

And shar-kata didn't work against the mosasaur's armored hide, so Gray couldn't hurt him . . .

. . . from the outside.

What Gray hadn't tried was attacking from the *inside*. Not totally inside since Grimkhan's mouth wasn't *entirely* closed around him, but Gray was staring down the mosasaur king's gullet and that was close enough.

It was all or nothing. This would work or he would be eaten.

Gray's shield flattened, and he could feel the dagger spikes on the roof of the monster's mouth touch his back. He gathered power until he felt as if he would explode into a fireball and then released it.

The pressure on his back stopped.

Gray couldn't hear anything from inside Grimkahn's gullet.

For a moment everything was silent.

Then the mosasaur's mouth disintegrated into charred pieces, falling to each side of Gray.

After a moment blood gushed forth from where Grimkahn's head used to be and the ocean around him turned red.

The rest of the mosasaur king's body crashed onto the seabed.

Grimkahn was finally dead.

CHAPTER 26

GRAY HOPED THE DEATH OF THEIR LEADER would cause the jurassic horde to stop fighting.

It was a false hope.

If anything, the monsters became more enraged. Grimkahn wasn't lying when he told Gray about his standing order to wipe them out. They would have to win this outright.

With the addition of the Hideg Shiver sharkkind from the Arktik and at least three or four battle pods of orcas from Icingholme Shiver, the tide had turned. Frilled sharks started swimming the Sparkle Blue at a faster pace. And the bladefish were deadly against the mosasaurs. They too, were dying. But there were still at least thirty of the giants left, along with several hundred frilled sharks.

They could have escaped if they wanted to, but instead they drove deeper into the Riptide United forces, inflicting huge casualties. Gray powered back into the melee. He rammed a frill away from an AuzyAuzy mariner and then bit the tail off another.

Gray saw Xander die in the fighting. Another of his friends was gone. The mariners he commanded slowed for a split second, unsure what to do. The swarm of frills and three mosasaurs they battled ripped into them.

The entire Indi and AuzyAuzy force was about to be annihilated. Gray whipped himself into the diamond-head. "To me!" he shouted. "Triple Tail Turns Up and Left!" Thankfully one of Olph's battle dolph cousins was there to click-razz the order so everyone could hear it.

The move swung their force over and crashed it into the weak side of this section of the jurassic horde. But the frilled sharks were quick to adjust and soon it was bloody, snout-to-snout, close combat again. Sharkkind and frills thrashed every which way, dying. One mosasaur was taken out by Salamanca. He sliced the beast's guts out from underneath while another swordfish drove its sharp bill deep into a mosasaur's eye socket to the brain. It sank, flippers jerking and twitching.

But still, sharkkind all around Gray died.

A shiver of terror crept down his spine. Even without Grimkahn the jurassic horde could win. They were driven by an almost psychotic madness to kill everyone around them.

And we don't have any more friends left who can show up and help, Gray thought as he avoided a wild tail strike from a frill.

Suddenly the frilled sharks were compacted against his mariners.

Unable to move freely, they became easier targets. Gray thought it was the orcas pushing forward, as the figures in the hazy red waters were larger than sharks.

They were swimming upright, though, with long necks.

They looked like prehistores but were sending frills and mosasaurs to the Sparkle Blue.

As they got closer he saw they were giant sea dragons.

Gray couldn't believe it.

Yappy's cousins from the Dark Blue had finally arrived.

The giant sea dragons were used to swimming where the water was thick and heavy, so in these higher depths they were lightning fast and more than a match for the frills. They were also big enough that three or four of them could take down a mosasaur.

Still, the jurassic horde didn't relent. They fought and died to the last.

When it was over there was a great cheer and then silence as the survivors took in a sight no one would ever wipe from their mind. The dead and dying formed a twenty and thirty foot deep pile on the seabed.

It was horrifying.

Gray felt guilty when a spasm of *relief* washed through him.

He was alive, the battle had been won, and the war was over.

AFTER-MATH

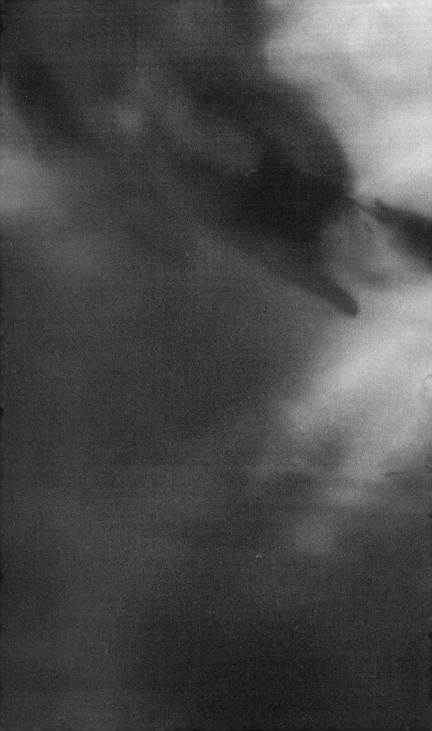

CHAPTER 27

THE BODIES OF THE FALLEN HAD TO BE moved after what would forever be called the Battle of Fathomir. The honored dead of Riptide, AuzyAuzy, Indi, Vortex, Hammer, Hideg, Icingholme, and all the smaller shivers that had fought were placed in one location while the jurassics were dragged to another. Thankfully a fierce current surged through the area for three days after the battle and helped the process. Even the mosasaurs were taken far enough away— with much help from Yappy's giant sea dragon cousins—so the living didn't have to be reminded of their evil and smell their stink.

Out of those piles of dead, life did spring. In short order entire new reefs were created from the bodies. They burst forth with thick greenie, corals, and whole new ecosystems.

It was the way of the Big Blue.

It seemed even if you swam the Sparkle Blue, you still had a job to do.

Gray swam out to speak in front of the Fathomir home and battle waters. A hundred thousand sharkkind and dwellers waited for his words. He had sent dozens of quickfin messengers to call representatives from every shiver they could think of, with Judijoan, Leilani, and BenzoBenzo, the huge blowfish head of the AuzyAuzy Eyes and Ears, being a tremendous help there.

Gray had already told the closest of his advisors what he would say to the gathered. That discussion, which included old friends and loved ones like his mother, Barkley, Snork, Striiker, Onyx, Jaunt, and new friends like Leilani, Tydal, Salamanca, Aleeyoot, BenzoBenzo, and Judijoan, was one of the rowdiest he had ever seen.

They were shocked and some disagreed, but he had made up his mind.

Gray would give up the title of Seazarein Emprex.

When he swam to a place where everyone could see him, there was a thunderous cheer. Gray called forth the energy of the waters to amplify his voice.

"I am Graynoldus Rex the Seazarein Emprex of the seven seas and all the oceans," he began, and the crowd quieted to listen. "As you might have guessed, it's a big job. I tried to do it as well as I could. Unfortunately we had to fight two wars in the short time I've been in charge."

Someone shouted, "And you won!" This set off another rousing cheer.

Gray waved his tail for order and the crowd quieted. "Despite the fact that we won—and it was *we* who won, not me—many of our friends and loved ones swam the Sparkle Blue before their time. Though it seemed that both of these wars were unavoidable, I'd like to try something different, something that may let us avoid future wars. I propose sharing the power between the shivers of the Big Blue. I want to form an assembly where shivers big and small can work together and more importantly, listen to the sharkkind, dwellers, and even those from the Underwaters and Dark Blue, so that there can be understanding between everyone. I want to stop wars before they start."

The crowd was hushed as they thought about this radical concept. The Five in the Line had been around since the time of Tyro. Gray was replacing it with a structure where power would be shared by many shivers. It was a big deal.

"By banding together, this oceanwide alliance would prevent not only bloodshed but also injustices committed by shivers who decide to use the fact that they are bigger and stronger to do evil. Each shiver will choose a representative to send to Fathomir and form this assembly. Yes, there will be a leader because I've learned you can't run a meeting without someone being in charge. But the leader wouldn't make the decisions, only guide the process. The assembly will vote on what to do *together*."

Out of the Riptide armada a chant began, softly at first but then gaining strength as more and more picked up the chant. Soon the waters thundered with, "GRAY-FOR-LEADER! GRAY-FOR-LEADER! GRAY-FOR-LEADER!"

Gray used his shar-kata and a slash of his tail to say, "NO!"

This hushed the crowd and even startled a few. "I apologize for raising my voice but I'm retiring not only the title of Seazarein Emprex but from any leadership role." A dismayed moan rolled through the gathered fins and dwellers. "I want the Big Blue to have a brand new start and I'm too connected with the old ways."

There were shouts of "No!" "We need you!" and "Please be our king!"

"Wait! Wait!" Gray told everyone and they once more strained to listen. "I don't want to leave you without any guidance, though. I'll be the Seazarein a little while longer until we get the process going and I'll even give you my choice for who should be leader of what I'll name the First Assembly of Fathomir."

Gray glanced at his advisors, giving Barkley a special grin.

There was one thing that he hadn't told his oldest and best friend during that loud meeting from before. He faced the crowd again and was pretty sure he heard Barkley say, "Gray, wait a second, what are you doing?"

"I nominate one of the smartest, bravest, and most kind sharks I know to be the first First Assembly leader of Fathomir—BARKLEY!"

"BARK-LEY! BARK-LEY! BARK-LEY! BARK-LEY! BARK-LEY!"

Gray swam to his friends and gave Barkley a nudge. "You always said you wanted more say in how things went."

"Actually I don't think I did!" Barkley said as the crowd continued to chant his name even louder. Then his friend became bashful. "I—I don't know. The job is so . . . big."

"I think it's a great choice!" Striiker exclaimed.

"Don't go laughing too hard, chowderhead," Barkley said. "If I'm elected, you're the new captain of the guardians."

"What? Aww, no!" Striiker replied before he nodded in acceptance. "Good one."

Gray flicked his tail at his closest friends and allies. "You'll all be playing large roles in the assembly. You can share the work together."

"But what about you, Gray?" asked Leilani. "What are you going to do?"

"I don't know yet," he said. "But when I do, you'll be the first to know."

Then Gray went to see the one important fish that hadn't been able to come to his speech.

Barkley couldn't believe it. He was leader of the Big Blue.

A dogfish!

The crowd continued to chant "Barkley! Barkley! Barkley!"

They didn't mind him being a dogfish one bit.

Maybe I should finally stop thinking like that, he thought.

It was a new day in the Big Blue.

A fresh beginning for everyone.

Anyone could be anything . . .

Barkley went over to Velenka, who was off to the side and by herself, not with the group of Gray's closest friends and advisors.

"What are you doing?" she asked, momentarily uneasy. "Don't you have to make a speech or something?"

"There will be time for speeches later," he told her. "I wouldn't be alive if it wasn't for you. You wanted a new start? Well, here it is. I'll need a fin that isn't afraid to tell me what they think even if they disagree. I want you to be my assistant and advisor. Are you up for the task?"

Even with the waters vibrating from the crowd

chanting his name, Barkley heard Velenka say, "Thank you with all my heart."

Barkley gave the mako a pat on the flank. "It also doesn't hurt to have someone sneaky when we're dealing with the more devious fins, now does it?"

"Oh *that* I can help with," Velenka said, her big black eyes sparkling.

CHAPTER 28

GRAY SWAM TO THE SMALL CAVERN, double-checking that he wasn't being followed. This wasn't easy, as seemingly everyone in the Big Blue wanted to wish him well. He had done things in his life that had scared him witless before. But this swim—this short distance inside the Fathomir strong point where he was perfectly safe—filled him with more dread than anything he'd done before.

It would be the last time he saw Takiza.

Gray got inside the secluded cave and saw Oceania, the surgeonfish.

"How is he?"

"I don't think he'll regain consciousness," she said, shaking her head sadly. "He's not in any pain, though."

His master had been placed on a rock shelf, and the light current caused his frilly fins to flutter nicely.

But his eyes were blank, with none of their usual sparkle, and his skin was grayish.

Takiza was dying.

"Can I have a minute alone?" Gray asked as tears sprang from his eyes.

"Of course," Oceania answered and swam from the chamber.

Gray hated to see his teacher this way. If he had a wish it would be to speak with the betta just one more time. He would have traded much for that.

"Hello Takiza," he said to the betta's unmoving form. "It's me, Gray. You know, the chowderhead you turned from a dumb pup into a shar-kata master. I wanted to tell you that we won. The ocean is safe and it wouldn't have happened without you." Gray's tears stung his eyes inside the small cavern. "You can rest now."

Gray wondered if Takiza could hear anything. In the end, he knew his words were more for himself than his Shiro. "I'd like to thank you for everything. You've made me the best shark I could be. I never knew my dad, Takiza, but I'd like to think he was like you. And on the day I swim the Sparkle Blue, if it's not too much trouble, I'd want you to come and greet me. Thanks, and rest easy, Takiza."

Gray left the cavern blinded by his tears. Once outside, a few of his friends motioned for him to join the celebration that was rapidly taking over the Fathomir homewaters. Gray gave them a fin waggle and burst away.

He wanted to be alone.

In the quiet of the golden greenie fields outside the Fathomir caverns, Gray found himself thinking of all the friends and loved ones he had lost since he left home in the Caribbi Sea with Barkley. The list was so long it broke his heart: Mari and Shell from Rogue Shiver; Atlas, Quickeyes, and Overbiter who had led Coral; King Lochlan, Xander, and Kendra from AuzyAuzy Shiver; Silversun and Grinder of Vortex and Hammer; Whalem of Indi; the captain of his guardians, Shear.

And soon Takiza.

Gray would try to concentrate on the good times and the amazing things they had done. He hoped that in the future the Big Blue would swim a new course and fewer sharks and dwellers would feel the sting of this kind of loss.

Gray sadly snapped at a mackerel that got close to his mouth, but missed.

The missed strike saved his life as Hokuu's spiked tail creased the top of his head.

If Gray hadn't gone after the fish, the spike surely would have blasted into his brain. He rolled a turn to the side and saw Hokuu, with an evil grin on his face and glowing with power.

"I should thank that fish," the frill said. "Your

death would have been too quick. This way I can really enjoy it!"

"We'll see about that," Gray said, grinding his teeth so hard he drew his own blood. He darted forward with a boost of shar-kata speed to snout ram Hokuu into next week.

The frilled shark easily avoided the attack.

Hokuu was even faster than usual and glowed a sickly green color. "You're still fat and slow I see," he said, and then laughed.

Gray hated the sound and went straight at the evil monster. He then stopped and whipped his tail around, scoring a solid tail slap that drove Hokuu backward.

The frill glared.

"Not so funny anymore?" Gray asked.

"No, you're still a joke," Hokuu said, his emerald eyes glittering with hate. "And your big stupid speech? I want you to know it means nothing! After I finish you I'm going to tear down everything you've planned. You may have killed Grimkahn, but he was a minnow compared to me. I could have wiped out both of your armadas together! But the fact is I loved watching you destroy each other. And because of that, it'll be that much easier for me to take absolute control."

Hokuu came forward, lightning fast, and plunged his spiked tail into Gray's lower flank. It didn't hurt. It felt like a tap when Riprap or Ebbie gave him their version of a snout ram. It felt okay, so Gray wasn't worried.

Still, there was an awful lot of blood clouding the water.

"I will kill every one of your friends, all those you hold dear," Hokuu said. "I'll save your mother . . . for last."

That was it. With a battle cry, Gray roared at his enemy.

He tried every move he could think of and even a few he invented on the spot.

Nothing worked.

Hokuu carved him to bits with his tail and tri-tipped teeth.

After Gray lost half his left fin, the frill unleashed a spiked tail strike into his left gills. Gary shook his head, trying to clear whatever was stuck in there. He could barely breathe.

Then he realized there wasn't anything blocking his left gills.

They were ripped to shreds on that side.

"And so it ends," Hokuu said as Gray drifted help-lessly in the water.

The frilled shark tapped Gray on the forehead with his pointy tail. "Ready to lose for good? One, two . . . " Hokuu drew back his tail as far as it would go. "Three!"

Then Hokuu disappeared.

At least, that's what it seemed like to Gray.

Hokuu had been shoved twenty yards to the side.

The frilled shark whirled and exclaimed, "What?"

"You always were an overconfident fool, Hokuu," Takiza said.

TAKIZA! thought Gray, although he could only gasp, "Ta-ki-za," in a breathy whisper.

"Yes," said the betta to Gray. "I was in a deep healing meditation, but your tears were so annoying I could not continue, so here I am."

"Enough of this, Nulo!" Hokuu said, coming forward. "You were never my match, even before I mastered dark-kata. You will die! And what could be better than killing you in front of your precious apprentice's eyes before I eat his heart?"

The fight between Takiza and Hokuu was so blindingly fast that Gray couldn't follow it. He wanted to help but was too injured to do anything but keep sinking as he lost blood. The light dimmed around Gray but he knew the sun wasn't going down. He was dying.

"How—how can you be keeping up?" spat Hokuu. "You don't use dark-kata!"

"Correct," Takiza said as he blocked another fiery attack from Hokuu. "I would never do anything so evil. But for every wicked current, there is a matching one of light."

Hokuu slashed at Takiza with his spiked tail, the high-pitched metallic whine from each attack running together into a single, continuous moan, they were so fast. "I see!" cried Hokuu with delight. "This is your last fight!"

For a moment Gray didn't understand but then it came to him. Takiza had filled himself with shar-kata power and was mixing it with what was left of his own life force.

"All I have to do is wait!" Hokuu said, withdrawing twenty yards. "I can come back when you're dead!"

"You could," said Takiza, glowing less now. "That is the coward's way and you are nothing if not a coward. But then . . . you will *never* have defeated me, Hokuu. I would remain unbeaten, despite your best efforts, and you will remember that *forever*."

This enraged Hokuu beyond anything Gray had ever seen. He fired blast after blast at the wispy betta, who was always a bit too quick. They streaked back and forth, trading places and attacks, firing energy bolts and blasts.

The waters thrummed with the thundering reports from their battle.

Then Takiza paused. His fins drooped.

With an eager glint in his eye Hokuu rushed forward. He shouted, "Victory is mine!" and used his Hurling Grace vomit attack, engulfing Takiza.

But at the same time, Takiza zoomed ahead, releasing a blade of light that seemed to pass by Hokuu but not stop him.

The vomit dripped off the betta's shield, leaving some stuck on his fragile body. This sent wispy, smoke-filled bubbles toward the chop-chop as it burned into his skin.

"You see?" Hokuu panted in short breaths to Gray. "I win. Now for you!"

Hokuu swam forward . . .

Well, half of Hokuu swam forward . . . and *away* from his lower body.

The frilled shark looked back at the fifteen feet of his body that was no longer connected.

Then blood poured from each of the severed ends.

"What?" asked Hokuu in bewilderment as he began sinking.

"The truth is," Takiza began. "You were my match only in your own mind."

Then Takiza glowed bright for a moment and launched a white-hot ball of fire at Hokuu.

It hit the frilled shark, and he died screaming before being totally incinerated.

His ashy remains washed away with the current, and it was like he had never existed.

Gray struggled to join Takiza, who was barely breathing and drifted in the water. "Are you okay?"

The betta regarded him with a haughty look. "Do I seem *okay*?"

Gray began to laugh and cry at the same time. The betta smiled. "Stop your unsightly weeping.

Swimming the Sparkle Blue will be a kindness. I am so very tired."

"No, no, no," was all Gray could say.

"Listen to me!" Takiza demanded. "I am not done teaching and time is short. If you ever come up against a situation that is too great for even you, you must find a quickfin." Takiza coughed. The bubbling vileness that Hokuu sprayed was working its way deep into his body.

"Quickfin?"

"Do not interrupt!" Takiza said. "Should there come a time when instead of an armada, one fin with the strength of an armada is needed, find a quickfin— any will do—and say these words: 'Flashnboomer, Whorl Current, Brinicle.' The code is ancient and to my knowledge has never been used, but remember the words anyway."

"I'm not in charge anymore," Gray said.

Takiza smiled. "For now. But no one knows which way future currents shall flow. Perhaps the Big Blue isn't done with you yet."

"I'll remember the words, master," Gray said through the tears. The betta stared at him, waiting. "You want me to say them again, don't you?"

"Humor me," Takiza said, giving Gray a light tap with his fin.

"Flashnboomer, Whorl Current, Brinicle," he said.

"Very good, Gray. I go now to my friends and loved

ones. I go to be with my own mother and father, whom I have not seen in so many ages. I am proud to have been your Shiro. As to your words, which I heard while meditating, I never had a son . . . but if I did, I hope he would have been somewhat like you."

The betta's body then glowed with vibrant colors and transformed into a million multicolored sparkles.

Gray was sure he was seeing an illusion of the Sparkle Blue, but these lights weren't the pulsing blobs that came with that.

No, these lit up the ocean with dazzling color in a display that made Gray smile.

They circled and dove, looping and whizzing.

He could feel it distinctly.

Takiza was happy.

Gray was sure of it.

His own heavy heart lightened.

Then Takiza gave Gray one last gift.

The rainbow sparkles that the betta had become went into his body and through him.

This tickled something fierce and caused Gray to laugh, even though he didn't want to.

When the sparkles left his body, flaring away in every direction, his injuries were gone.

"Goodbye, Takiza," Gray said.

And with that Takiza Jaelynn Betta vam Delacrest Waveland ka Boom Boom swam the Sparkle Blue.

CHAPTER 29

"AND THAT'S HOW TAKIZA SAVED MY LIFE," Gray told everyone as he finished the story of the betta's battle with Hokuu.

Barkley, Leilani, Striiker, and Snork could scarcely believe their ears.

"Hokuu's dead," Barkley whispered. "It's over."

Snork shook his head. "I'm sad about Takiza but I know Salamanca is going to be mad. He really wanted to be the one to beat Hokuu."

"Everyone wanted to," Striiker nodded with approval. "But only one fish in all the wet world could do it. That Takiza was a great fin."

Leilani looked at Gray. "Are you all right?"

Gray flexed his fins up and down. The one that had been sliced off tickled but otherwise felt fine. "I am. I miss Takiza, but now that it's over it's like this huge weight has been lifted from me."

"Because you loaded it on me!" said Barkley, giving him a bump. His friend had been overwhelmingly chosen as the first-ever leader of the First Assembly of Fathomir.

"You had it coming," Gray said. "Not because I'm getting you back for anything, but because I think you're the best fish for the job."

"Really?" asked Barkley. "Not even a bit?"

"Maybe a little for all those fat jokes when we were pups."

Barkley nodded. "I do think the fins of the Big Blue are ready for a change, though. The right ideas could transform the seven seas! And I'll have help from a lot of smart fish; Tydal is Indi's representative, Jaunt has been chosen as AuzyAuzy's, Judijoan knows *everything*, and of course Striiker will be protecting my dorsal fin and also creating the Fathomir defense force."

Gray hadn't heard about this.

The great white whipped his tail from side to side eagerly. "Gonna be a lot of work but I can't wait. Remember how you combined Indi and AuzyAuzy into one fighting force after Finnivus was defeated? They worked together perfectly against Grimkahn, even though they used to be enemies. Well, I'd like to do that with *all* the ancient shivers. We rotate five hundred fins from each shiver into the armada and they train together. I mean, no one's gonna listen to the First Assembly unless its decisions are backed up by some teeth, right?"

Barkley took over, enthusiasm lighting up his eyes. "We'll have the most powerful force in the seas. That's good, but not the point. The important part is that sharkkind and dwellers from all over the ocean will get to know each other. When they go back to their home shivers they can say, 'Hey I met those fins from Indi Shiver. They're not the bloodthirsty crazy-fish we heard about; they're okay.'"

Leilani smiled. "That's a wonderful idea. You can stop prejudice and hate before it starts."

"See?" Gray said. "I knew I picked the right shark. Or at least I picked the shark that would pick all the other right sharks. Either way's good."

"I offered Leilani a position as an advisor but oddly she said no," Barkley told Gray, giving the spinner a calculating look. "She's being very secretive about what she's doing in the future. Do you know anything about that, Gray?"

"I'm right here, you know," Leilani said with a smile.

Gray opened his mouth to tell Barkley what they were going to do but was interrupted by a colorful blur—Yappy.

"Hey, it's Gray and Barkley! Barkley and Gray!" shouted the sea dragon as he waved his leafy flippers in excitement. "Didn't I tell you my cousins would come? And they're loads of fun. As long as you don't cheat at Tuna Roll. They don't like that at all. But I told you they'd come and they did!"

"They certainly did," said Gray.

"You did great, Yappy," Barkley agreed as he poked Gray with his tail. "Back to the previous topic. I think it's about time you tell us what you're going to be—"

Barkley didn't get to ask the rest of his question because Yappy blurted, "Hey Gray! Did you tell everyone how you're going to your old reef in the Caribbi Sea with Coral Shiver and all the other sharkkind who don't have a home?"

Barkley, Snork, and Striiker looked at Gray in surprise. Leilani was the only one that didn't. She was coming with him. It was why she hadn't taken a position in the First Assembly.

"No Yappy, I hadn't quite yet," Gray said with a grin.

"Oh, I'm sorry," Yappy said. "Did I spoil the surprise?"

"Not at all," Gray told him. "What do you think, Bark?"

Barkley flicked his fins up and down. "That's amazing! Is your mom going, too?"

Gray nodded. "She is, along with every orphan that lost their parents through the wars with Grimkahn and Finnivus, and any other small shivers that want a new start." Gray looked at each of his friends. "The place I grew up was destroyed by war. It feels right that it should be rebuilt by the survivors of this last one."

"I'm going for sure!" Yappy said. "What about you Barkley?"

"Well no, I guess I can't," said his friend.

Gray gave Barkley a slap to the flank. "Hey, who says the First Assembly leader doesn't go on listening tours around the oceans, including the Caribbi Sea?"

"That's right!" Barkley said. "It's very important to listen! You're a genius!"

"And *there's* something I've never been called," Gray said. Everyone laughed. He turned to Striiker and Snork. "Of course, you'll both be honorary members of Coral Shiver."

"I'm always up for visiting new places," said Striiker.

"Thanks, Gray," Snork said. "I'd love to come and see your home someday."

"But not today, tomorrow, or next week!" said Salamanca.

"It's Salamanca!" yelled Yappy. "Hey, Salamanca! What's it like to have a big nose like yours? Have you ever gotten it stuck in a rock? Or coral? How about especially thick greenie?"

Salamanca rolled his eyes when he saw Yappy. The sea dragon began pestering the other bladefish who were with the big marlin. Salamanca leaned in to Gray and Barkley and spoke low. "Salamanca does not know if you have noticed, but the sea dragon called Yappy is formidable at continuously speaking. He is a wonder of sorts."

"We might have noticed that," said Barkley with a grin.

Snork swished his tail. "I'll complete my training and then who knows? Maybe I'll be assigned to look after your shiver, or Fathomir."

"What's this?" asked Gray.

Salamanca nodded his long bill up and down. "The bladefish have become too secretive. We would like to be included in the various decisions made by this First Assembly of Fathomir."

"So Gray, what are you doing now?" asked Striiker.

"I believe we just covered that in detail," Barkley answered.

"No, I mean right this minute," the great white said. He flicked his tail toward the giant celebration in the golden greenie fields of Fathomir. "If none of us is doing anything too important maybe we could join the party for a bit?"

Everyone looked to Gray to make this one last decision for them, so he nodded. "That's an excellent idea. For my last decree as Seazarein Emprex, I *order* you all to have as much fun as possible for the next few days."

His friends cheered and everyone jammed together for a group rub before they swam over and joined the happy crowd.

They had earned it.

CORAL SHIVER

CHAPTER 30

PEACE HAD COME TO THE BIG BLUE. THE water was warm and it was a beautiful summer day with the sun shining down from the chop-chop. Gray looked out over the reef at Coral Shiver and sighed, content. He swam by Miss Lamprey, the eel school teacher at the reef, and her two assistants as they taught a class on navigation to hundreds of pups.

Coral Shiver was much larger than when he had been young. Many of the refugees had chosen to settle down with them. Gray had taken the position of leader but the day-to-day decisions he left to his mother, Sandy. Onyx had insisted on putting together a mariner force but the training wasn't as harsh as it was when they were at war. For that Gray was thankful.

"Do you miss it?" Leilani asked. She too was a teacher and specialized in helping the orphans who were most traumatized.

Gray looked at the spinner and smiled. Although he knew what she was referring to he asked, "Miss what?"

Leilani gave him a rub to the flank. "You know, being a part of all the big decisions."

"Nope," Gray said, waggling a fin. "Not even a little. Even when there's nothing going on, there's always something, and that's tiring. Besides, things are going fine."

Barkley was doing wonderfully. Velenka was his first advisor, and she had a knack for cunning negotiation. Maybe she'd be elected as assembly leader one day and in a way conquer the ocean like she always wanted. Other than a few minor territory disputes, the currents were smooth. Everything was being solved by talking rather than fighting, and that was a welcome change.

The First Assembly of Fathomir had voted that he be kept up on current events every week by quickfin messenger. Gray didn't mind getting updates but he didn't weigh in with his opinion unless specifically asked. Usually Barkley sent Eugene Speedmeister and it was always good to see the young flying fish. He had become a legend among the quickfins since his wild swim to the Arktik.

Gray shuddered to think what would have happened in the battle against Grimkahn without Hideg and Icingholme Shivers' help. And AuzyAuzy's, and

Indi's, and Hammer's, and Vortex's, and Yappy's cousins, and even the mysterious and perfectly timed school of jellyfish that floated through the battle courtesy of Trank, although he denied it every time he was asked.

If even one of them hadn't shown up . . .

Gray banished the thought.

They had all come. The war had been won.

Gray had seen Tydal a month ago, when an official Indi Shiver delegation visited Coral Shiver. They had eaten and talked and watched many rounds of Tuna Roll. Gray even got to join in for a few games. That was fun. It was the first-ever official visit to Coral, and Barkley was miffed that it wasn't him doing the visiting. His friend was due to arrive in a month, when his schedule cleared. That was one of the numerous problems with being an important leader. Your time was never your own.

No, Gray didn't miss it.

Suddenly there was a commotion at the far end of the reef.

Leilani gave Gray a look. "What could that be?"

"Let's go check it out," he said and they swam to the disturbance.

"If you ever do it again I'll give you each such a fin slap that you won't stop spinning for a week!" Onyx yelled.

"Aww, come on!" protested Riprap. "We were only having fun! The reef is boring!"

Ebbie looked to Sandy with her big eyes. "We weren't far away, Mom. And it's not even dark."

Gray and Leilani joined them. "So what's this?" he asked.

Sandy gave them an amused grin. "It seems these two were attracted by a drove of bluefin tuna and ended up two miles away by the time they were done chasing it."

"One of our patrols found them," added Onyx.

"That sounds oddly familiar," Gray said. He had done the same thing with Barkley. It got him banished from Coral Shiver and began his long journey into the open waters. Of course, they didn't need to fear being discovered by hostile sharkkind like in the old days. Coral was the largest shiver in the area and their neighbors were peaceful.

"I don't think we have to call a council meeting," Onyx said to Gray. "Since you have experience with this kind of thing, you can decide their punishment."

"You're not going to banish us, are you?" asked Riprap.

"Don't banish us, Gray!" said Ebbie. "We like it here!"

"No one's being banished," he told the two. "But the rules are in place for a reason and you broke them. You're grounded for a week."

Ebbie shook her head. "That's so unfair."

"A whole week?" sputtered Riprap. "We thought you were cool!"

"Hey, I'm still cool," Gray said with a smile.

Sandy pushed the little sharks toward the reef with her tail. "Go on, you two." Sandy looked at him as she followed. "Not so great when you're the one in charge of the punishing, is it?"

Gray nodded at Sandy. "Sometimes that's the way it goes. But I'm not that mature yet, either." He called after his brother and sister. "Why don't we play some hide and seek? You guys hide and Leilani and I will seek. But stay near the reef!"

"Totally cool!" cried Riprap.

"You'll never find us," said Ebbie, and both sharks swam off.

Onyx gave Gray a fin waggle. "It's time to check how our mariners do in a surprise drill."

"Try not to be too hard on them," Gray said. Thinking better of this he added, "But make sure they learn."

Onyx left Gray and Leilani to hover in the refreshing current. They looked out over the reef and all the shiver sharks.

"This is nice," she said.

"I could get used to it," Gray answered. "I think it'll be smooth currents from here on out."

"So, should we go find Riprap and Ebbie?" asked Leilani.

Gray was about to say yes when he saw something in the distance. It was moving fast and straight at them. It was Eugene Speedmeister. The flying fish was totally out of breath by the time he got to them. "Oh, thank Tyro I found you! You have to come!" Eugene said. "The First Assembly needs you!"

"What's the message?" asked Leilani.

Eugene flicked his fins up and down in a salute. "Message to the last Seazarein Emprex Graynoldus from First Assembly Leader Barkley. Code word, Octopi. The message is as follows: 'The jellies are threatening to go to war and they'll only talk with you. Please come as soon as possible.'"

"The jellyfish want to go to war?" said Leilani, not believing the words as they came from her mouth.

Gray sighed and looked at the spinner. "Well, looks like I jinxed it."

Apparently the Big Blue wasn't quite done with him yet.

Then Gray heard something on the current.

It sounded remarkably like Takiza laughing.

THE END . . . FOR NOW

ACKNOWLEDGMENTS

First I'd like to thank Ben Schrank, president and publisher of Razorbill, who took a huge chance by letting a first-time author write this book series.

Also in the Penguin family, thanks to Emily Romero, Erin Dempsey, Shanta Newlin, Scottie Bowditch, Courtney Wood, Lisa Kelly, Anna Jarzab, Elizabeth Zajac, Mia Garcia, Tarah Theoret, and everyone else from marketing, publicity, and sales. My hardworking design and production team: Vivian Kirklin in managing editorial, Kristin Smith in design, and Amy White in production. And special thanks to Laura Arnold and Rebecca Kilman, my fantastic editors and fintastic conspirators on all things Shark Wars.

I'd also like to thank Wil Monte and his talented crew at Millipede Creative Development, led by Jason Rawlings, for creating the Shark Wars game. I hope to one day meet you lot in Melbourne for a pint. Thanks to illustrator Martin Ansin for the Shark Wars covers and endpapers, which look better than I could have ever imagined; and my new agent Alec Shane at Writers House. Also thanks to Ken Wright, my old agent and now newly minted Vice President and Publisher of Viking Children's Books. Best of luck and thanks for your help.

To my good friend Jim Krieg, who has done so much that I can never repay him, although that doesn't mean I won't try. And finally to my family and friends who were so supportive through the years. Best wishes to you all.

Sharpen your shark senses with:

- 8 challenging levels that put your skills to the ultimate test: hunt droves of slippery tuna and lightning-fast lobsters, fight killer crabs and hostile intruders, test your underwater navigation and swim speed, battle the rival sharks of Razor Shiver, and much more!
- Control options: joystick or tilt-to-swim
- Play as Gray or his best friend Barkley
- Hundreds of hidden objects and treasure
- Game Center leaderboards to challenge friends and outrank the world
- Updates on all the latest Shark Wars news and events
- The ultimate guide to the book series' main characters and shark clans

Download the FREE Shark Wars App at SharkWarsSeries.com

Razorbill · An Imprint of Penguin Group (USA) Inc.

EJ ALTBACKER is a screenwriter who has worked on television shows including *Green Lantern: The Animated Series*, *Ben 10*, *Mucha Lucha*, and *Spider-Man*. He lives in Hermosa Beach, California.

Visit **www.SharkWarsSeries.com** to learn more and to play the Shark Wars game!

31901055352167

THE FINAL BATTLE